At ten thousand miles, the sound started up: the lost, lonely wail of air molecules being split by a couple thousand tons of overaged tramp freighter, coming in too fast, on a bad track, with no retros working. I played with what was left of the attitude jets, jockeying her around into a tail-first position, saving the last of my reaction mass for when and where it would do the most good. When I had her where I wanted her, I had less than eight thousand miles of gravity to work with. I checked the plotting board, pin-pointing my target area, while she bucked and buffeted under me and the moans rose to howls like gut-shot dire-beasts.

At two hundred miles, the drive engines cut in and everything turned to whirly red lights and pressures like a toad feels under a boot. That went on long enough for me to pass out and come to half a dozen times. Then suddenly she was tumbling in free fall and there were only seconds left. Getting a hand on the pod release was no harder than packing an anvil up a rope ladder; I felt the shock as the cargo section blasted free and away. I got myself into the drop suit, and into position in the escape pod, clamped the shock frame down, took a last lungful of stale ship air, and slapped the eject button. Ten tons of feather pillow hit me in the face and knocked me into another world.

Other books by Keith Laumer
available from TOR:

KEITH LAUMER

ONCE THERE WAS A GIANT

TOR

A TOM DOHERTY ASSOCIATES BOOK

For Ginnie, the mother of my
grandson, Christopher Michael.

A TOR Book
Published by: Tom Doherty Associates,
8-10 West 36th Street,
New York, N.Y. 10018

First TOR printing, July 1984

ISBN: 0-812-54371-8
CAN. ED.: 0-812-54372-6

Cover art by Dave Maddingly

Printed in the United States of America

ONCE THERE
WAS A GIANT

CHAPTER ONE

It was one of those self-consciously raunchy dives off Cargo Street that you can find in any port town in the Arm, serving the few genuine dockwallopers and decayed spacemen that liked being stared at by tourists, plus the tourists, but mostly the sharpies or would-be sharpies that preyed on both brands of sucker. I came in with just enough swagger to confuse the issue: which kind was I? There was that subtle rearrangement of conversational groups as the company present sorted themselves out into active participants and spectators, relatively few of the latter. I saw my mark right away, holed up in a corner booth with a couple of what he probably thought were tough guys. All three swiveled their heads in a leisurely way long enough to show me matched insolent snickers. Then one of the side-boys rapped on the table and rose; he said something to the mark, an ex-soldier named Keeler, and pushed off for the bar, which put him behind me. The mark made a production of not looking at me as I worked my way over to his corner, while appearing to be a little bewildered by it all. I fetched up at his table just in time to get jostled by hard boy number two, just getting up. I gave him an uncertain grin for his trouble, and took his still-warm seat, opposite Keeler. The hard case drifted away, muttering. That left me and Keeler, face to face.

"—if you don't mind," I was saying when he poked a finger at my chest and said, "Beat it, bum." in a voice as friendly as a slammed door.

I sat tight and took a good look at him. I knew a little more about this mark, more personal detail, that is, because twenty years before he had been the paid-off lieutenant who had let a Mob ship through his section of the Cordon to raid the mining camp on Ceres where I had been spending my time growing up to the age of twelve. I remember wondering "twelve what?" and not quite understanding why it had something to do with the number of times one of the brighter nearby stars—the double one, really a planet—went from left of the sun to right and back again, which seemed pretty screwy to me. Bombeck and his raiders hadn't left much of Extraction Station Five, but a few of us kids hid in an old cutting and came out after the shooting was over. Well, time does strange things, and now I was Baird Ulrik, licensed assassin, and Keeler was my current contract. Well, it's a living.

2

It's not often a fellow gets paid well to do what he'd like to do for free, and it made a lot of difference. No contract man can afford to be picky, but I had always made it a point to accept contracts only on marks that I agreed needed killing: Dope-runners, con-men, rabble-rousers-for-money, and the like, of which there was an adequate supply to keep our small but elite cadre of licensed operators busy. When Keeler came along, I tried not to look too eager, to keep the price up. It wasn't any life-long dream of mine, to get the man responsible for the slaughter of what passed for my family, including burning the old homestead with them in it, alive or dead, nobody knew—but I thought there was a certain elegance, as the math boys say, to my being the one to end his career for him. After he was cashiered, he'd signed on with the Mob, and worked his way up to top son-of-a-bitch for this part of the Ring. Maybe you're surprised that it made any difference to a hardened killer, but I'd never really gotten much satisfaction out of my work, because it came too easy to me. Sure, I'm a contract killer—and if not proud of it, at least not ashamed of it. Like they say, it's a

9

tough, lonely, dirty job—but someone has to do it. It's really a lot more civilized to give the condemned man a gun, if he wants one, and let him run as far as he likes, to exercise his instinct for self-preservation, rather than locking him up on Death Row to wait for an impersonal death by machine, like I understand they used to do in more barbaric times. Keeler knew he had it coming to him, but not when, or how, or by whom. He'd find out soon enough; I didn't keep him in suspense.

"Don't kid me, Keeler." I told him. "Do you want it right here in front of all your friends, or shall we take a little walk?"

"You wouldn't dare," he hoped aloud. "Buck is right behind you, and Barney's watching, don't ever doubt it."

"Sure, you have to speak your lines, Keeler," I conceded, "but you know better." Then he fooled me: he had more gall than I'd figured. He got up and walked away, and Barney and Buck closed in, front and back, and off they went, with everybody looking from them to me. Just as they reached the door I called after them:

"Buck and Barney, better hit the deck fast," and I fired from under the table close enough to Buck's ear to lend substance to my suggestion. Keeler looked as alone as the last tree in the woods when the timber harvesters finish, but he did his snappy hip-draw and I let him put two hard slugs into the paneling behind me before I got up and went over and took it away from him. He gibbered a little and tried to wrestle, but after I broke his arm the fight went out of him. Then he tried to deal, and that disgusted me and I got a little angry and broke his neck, almost accidentally.

3

Barney and Buck seemed a little uncertain about what to do next, after they'd gotten up and dusted themselves off, so I told them to get rid of Keeler in a discreet way, because even though my license has the endorsement that allows me to clam up in self-defense, I'd still had to stand trial and prove necessity. I always avoid that kind of publicity, so I shoved them out of my way and went out into the rutted street and along to the cracked and peeling plastic facade of the formerly (a *very* long time ago) tourist-elegant hostelry, done in the Early Delapidated Miami Beach style, and holed up in my quarters to think about my next move. I was just getting adjusted to the lumps in the sawdust mattress when the boys in blue arrived. They pointed some guns at me and told me they were Special Treasury cops, and showed me little gold badges to prove it. After they finished the room they told me not to leave town, that they'd have a fishy eye on me and, oh yes, to watch myself. While I was working on a snappy answer to that one, they left. They seemed to be in a hurry. The visit bothered me a little because I couldn't figure what it was for, so I gave it up and got a few hours' sleep.

Before dawn, about two hours later, I was at the broken-down ops shed, clearing my shore-boat, which went fast because I'd taken the time to put on the old uniform I kept in my foot-locker for such occasions. It was all "Yes, sir, Cap'n, sir." and "anything more I can do for you, sir?" A line captain still impresses the yokels in all those border towns. I made it to my bucket, which that year happened to be a converted ex-Navy hundred-ton light destroyer, and by the time I had unpacked, and downed a number-three-ration lunch, I was on track for home, with the job done, my hard-earned quarter-mil waiting, and not a care in the world. Just after I cleaned the disposal unit and reset it, feeling about as good as anybody in my profession ever gets to feel, they hit me.

It was only a mild jolt of EMS, that didn't even heat the brass buttons on my fancy suit, but it put my tub into a tumble and blew every soft circuit aboard. I made it to the special manual-hydraulic-combustion panel I'd had installed very quietly at one of the best hot-drops on Callisto, and prepared my little surprise. The primitive optic fibre periscope showed me a stubby black fifty-tonner with the gold-and-blue blazon of the Special Treasury cops holding station parallel to my axis of spin and about a hundred yards away. Two men were on the way across, using the very latest in fail-safe EVA units, and towing a heavy-duty can opener, so I opened up before they could use the cutter, and was looking at the same pair who'd frisked my room back on Little C.

They were almost polite about it; it seemed they took my blue suit seriously, called me "Captain" ten times in five minutes. They didn't waste a lot

of time on preliminaries, just went directly to the
cargo access hatch and broke the lock on it before
I could key it, and after a good ten seconds inside,
came out and told me my rights. It seems they'd
found a load of the pink stuff that would have half
the population of the System yodelling Pagliacci
from the top of the nearest flagpole if it were
evenly distributed. Now I knew what they'd been
in a hurry to do after their informal call at my flop.

I explained that it was all just one of those
snafus, that I must have gotten somebody else's
baggage by mistake, but they weren't listening.
Instead, two more glum-looking fellows arrived,
and after a very brief conference, they went to my
quarters and straight to the shore-pack I'd had with
me on Ceres, and came up with an envelope full of
documents that proved that I had bought and paid
for the dope in the open market on Charon, about
three weeks before I had been released from the
hospital at Pluto Station. I told them about my
alibi, and they checked a little and the boss cop, a
skinny, big-nosed little bantam they called Mr.
Illini, took me aside.

"Why a man in your position would think you
could sneak a load in past us, is beyond me," he
confided. "You know as well as I do, Captain,
that we've got the Inner Line sealed with the best
equipment there is. No way can a tub like this get
by us. Get your stuff, we're going in to Mars Four
to book you. And by the way, are you really
Navy? If so, it seems you blew your retirement,
pal."

It seemed the boys had something in mind, so I
didn't spring my little surprise, but let them take
me in tow.

4

Along the way, Illini gave me the dirt in small doses, starting with some cultural orientation on an extra-solar planet called Vangard, an almost-but-not-quite Earth-type in a lonely orbit out near Alpha, and all about how the first colonists had almost made it, in spite of a few problems like low G, so they had to learn to walk all over again, and an average surface temperature well below the freezing point of H_2O, and all that. Seems the low G had the effect of confusing the body's growth control system, and the third generation males averaged nine feet in height, all in good proportion and fully functional, so the last few survivors hung on and stretched the original homestead rights past the three hundred year mark. "A damn shame," Illini told me: "A handful of oversized squatters sustaining a Class Four Quarantine that prevents proper development of all that territory! Territory we need, dammit!" He worked up a little righteous wrath, going over all this stuff that he knew I knew at least as well as he did; then he got to the point:

"Just one left," he said. "One man, one oversized clodhopper, and now they've raised the classification to Q-5! Not a damn thing we can do about it legally, Ulrik—but there are a few of us that think the needs of the human race take precedence. So—once this big fella is gone—Vangard is wide open. Need I say more?''

I was in no position to argue, even if I'd wanted to. They had me cold, and aside from the details of the planted dope and the planted papers, it was all perfectly legit. They were bona-fide T-men, and nobody, not even I, took jazreel-smuggling as a harmless, boyish prank.

I picked the right moment and tripped the master switch to cancel the surprise party for the boys, having decided I wasn't quite yet ready for suicide. They never knew how close they'd come. Well, it would have been a flashy exit, for all hands.

It wasn't a fun voyage home, but finally it was over, and they hustled me right along to jail, and the next day into court.

5

It wasn't a real courtroom, but that figured, because it wasn't a real court-martial, and a good thing, too. The load of pink stuff I'd been caught with would have gotten me cashiered, and life plus twenty in the big lockup at League Central, if the line-captain's uniform I'd been wearing hadn't been phony. Still, the boys weren't kidding, so I played along solemnly as they went through the motions, found me guilty as hell, and then got down to business.

"Baird Ulrik," the big fellow with the old-fashioned whiskers said in his big, official-sounding voice. "It is the judgment of this court that such disposal shall be made of you as is prescribed by itself."

"That means we do as we like with you, Ulrik," the smooth character who had been appointed my defense counsel said—the first time he had opened his mouth since the 'trial' began.

"It is therefore directed," Whiskers went on, not laughing, "that you shall suffer capital punishment, not in an orthodox manner, but in a fashion which will serve the public interest."

My counsel leaned close again. "That means we've got a use for you, Ulrik," he told me. "You're a lucky man: your valuable talent won't be wasted."

It took them another hour to come out with all the details; even to Boss Judd, willfully breaking a Class Five quarantine was sweaty business. And there was more:

"The public has a corny idea this big bum is some kind of noble hero, holding onto the ancestral lands all alone, against all the odds," my counsel summed up.

"Sure," I agreed. "That's old stuff, counselor; what's in it for the Mob?"

"There's no occasion to sneer," my lawyer told me. " 'Mob' is a long-outdated term. The Organization exercises, de facto, at least at much power as the so-called "legitimate" government, and has indeed been delegated the police and judicial functions here in the Belt, where the not-so-long arm of the Assembly can't reach.''

"Sure," I agreed. "These days, you can't hardly tell the hoods from the Forces of Righteousness. Well, maybe you never could. So what's it got to do with little old law-abiding me?"

"With Johnny Thunder dead—get that name some sob-sister hung on this slob—there's no legal basis for Q-5," the shyster told me. "That means a wide-awake developer can go in and stake a claim to two million squares of top quality real estate—and Boss don't sleep much."

"It's so silly it might work," I had to admit. "So when you couldn't hire me for the hit, you framed me with a half-million units of jazreel— and here I am, ready to do your dirty work."

"Don't knock it, Ulrik," Illini said smoothly. "It works."

And the dirty part of it was, he was absolutely right. I had no choice.

6

From a half-million miles out, Vangard was a sphere of gray cast-iron, arc-lit yellow-white on the sunward side, coal-mine black on the other, with a wide band of rust-red along the terminator. The mountain ranges showed up as crooked black hair-lines radiating from the white dazzle of the poles, fanning out, with smaller ridges rising between them, forming a band of broken gridwork across the planet like the back of an old man's hand. I watched the detail grow on the screen until I could match it up with the lines on the nav chart, and it was time to go into my routine. I broke the seal on my U-beamer and sounded my Mayday:

"King Uncle 629 calling XCQ! I'm in trouble! I'm on emergency approach to R-7985-23-D, but it doesn't look good. My track is 093 plus 15, at 19-0-8 standard, mark! Standing by for instructions, and make it fast! Relay, all stations!" The lines were corny, but at this point I had to follow the script. I set the auto-squawk to squirt the call out a thousand times in one-millisec bursts, then switched to listen and waited while forty-five seconds went past. That's how long it would take the hype signal to hit the beamer station of Ring 8 and bounce back an automatic AK.

The auto signal came in right on schedule; another half a minute passed in silence, and a cold finger touched my spine. Then a voice that sounded like I shouldn't have disturbed its nap came in:

"King Uncle 629, Monitor Station Z-448 reading you three by three. You are not, repeat *not* cleared for planetfall. Report full detail—"

"Belay that!" I came back with plenty of edge. "I'm going to hit this rock; how hard depends on you! Get me down first and we'll handle the paperwork later!"

"You're inside interdict range of a Class Five quarantined world. This is an official navigational notice to clear off—"

"Wise up, 448," I cut into that. "I'm seven hundred hours out of Dobie with a special cargo aboard! You think I *picked* this spot to fuse down? I need a tech advisory and I need it now!"

Another wait; then my contact came back on, sounding tight-lipped: "King Uncle, transmit a board read-out."

"Sure, sure. But hurry it up." I sounded rattled, which didn't require much acting ability, under the circumstances. Boss Judd didn't pay off on unavoidable mission aborts. I pushed the buttons that gave Z-448 a set of duplicate instrument readings that would prove I was in even worse trouble than I claimed. It was no fake. I'd spent plenty to make sure the old tub had seen her last port.

"All right, King Uncle; you waited too long to make your report, you're going to have to jettison cargo and set up the following nav sequence—"

"I said special cargo!" I yelled back at him. "Category ten! I'm on a contract run for the Dobie med service. I'm carrying ten freeze cases!"

"Uh, roger, King Uncle," the station came back, sounding a little off-balance now. "I understand you have living casualties under cryothesis aboard. Stand by." There was a pause. "You've handed me a cozy one, 629," the voice added, sounding almost human.

"Yeah," I said. "Put some snap on it. That rock's coming up fast."

I sat and listened to the star-crackle. A light and a half away, the station computer would be going into action, chewing up the data from my board and spitting out a solution; and meanwhile, the sharp boy on duty would be checking out my story. That was good. I wanted it checked. It was solid all down the line. The passengers lashed down in the cargo cell were miners, badly burned in a flash fire three months ago on Dobie, a mean little world with no treatment facilities. I was due to collect five million and a full pardon when I delivered them to the med center on Commonweal in a viable condition. My pre-lift inspection was on file, along with my flight plan, which would show my minimum-boost trajectory in past Vangard, just the way a shoestring operator would plot it, on the cheap. It was all in the record. I was legitimate, a victim of circumstances. It was their ball now. And if my calculations were any good, there was only one way they could play it.

"King Uncle, you're in serious trouble," my unseen informant told me. "But I have a possible out for you. You're carrying a detachable cargo pod?" He paused as if he expected an answer, then went on. "You're going to have to ride her down, then jettison the pod on airfoils inside atmosphere. Afterwards, you'll have only a few seconds in which to eject. Understood? I'll feed you the conning data now." A string of numbers rattled off to be automatically recorded and fed into the control sequencer.

"Understood, 448," I said when he finished. "But look—that's a wild country down there. Suppose the cooler's damaged in the drop? I'd better stay with her and try to set her down easy."

"Impossible, King Uncle!" The voice had warmed up a few degrees. After all, I was a brave though penny-pinching merchant captain, determined to do my duty by my charges even at the risk of my own neck.

"Frankly, even this approach is marginal," he confided. "Your one chance—and your cargo's—is to follow my instructions implicitly!" He didn't add that it was a criminal offense not to comply with a Monitor's navigational order. He didn't have to. I knew that, was counting on it.

"If you say so. I've got a marker circuit on the pod. But listen: how long will it take for you fellows to get a relief boat out here?"

"It's already on the way. The run will take . . . just under three hundred hours."

"That's over twelve standard days!" I allowed the short pause required for the slow mental process of a poor but honest spacer to reach some simple conclusions, then blurted: "If that freeze equipment's knocked out, the insulation won't hold low-0 that long! And . . ." Another pause for the next obvious thought to form. "And what about me? How do I stay alive down there?"

"Let's get you down first, Captain." Some of the sympathy had slipped, but not much. Even a hero is entitled to give some thought to staying alive, after he's seen to the troops.

There was little more talk, but the important things had all been said. I was following orders, doing what I was told, no more, no less. Inside the hour, the whole Tri-D watching public of the Sector would know that a disabled hospital ship was down on Vanguard, with ten men's lives—eleven, if you counted mine—hanging in the balance. And I'd be inside the target's defenses, in position for phase two.

7

At ten thousand miles, the sound started up: the lost, lonely wail of air molecules being split by a couple thousand tons of overaged tramp freighter, coming in too fast, on a bad track, with no retros working. I played with what was left of the attitude jets, jockeying her around into a tail-first position, saving the last of my reaction mass for when and where it would do the most good. When I had her where I wanted her, I had less than eight thousand miles of gravity well to work with. I checked the plotting board, pin-pointing my target area, while she bucked and buffeted under me and the moans rose to howls like gut-shot dire-beasts.

At two hundred miles, the drive engines cut in and everything turned to whirly red lights, and pressures like a toad feels under a boot. That went on long enough for me to pass out and come to half a dozen times. Then suddenly she was tumbling in free fall and there were only seconds left. Getting a hand on the pod release was no harder than packing an anvil up a rope ladder; I felt the shock as the cargo section blasted free and away. I got myself into the drop-suit and into position in the escape pod, clamped the shock frame down, took a last lungfull of stale ship air, and slapped the eject button. Ten tons of feather pillow hit me in the face and knocked me into another world.

8

I swam up out of the big, black ocean where the bad dreams wait and popped through into the watery sunshine of semi-consciousness in time to get a fast panoramic view of mountains like shark's teeth ranked in snow-capped rows that marched across the world to a serrated horizon a hundred miles away. I must have blacked out again, because the next second a single peak was filling the drop-suit's bull's-eye screen in front of my face, racing toward me like a breaking wave. The third time I came up, I realized I was on chutes, swaying down toward what looked like a tumbled field of dark lava. Then I saw that it was foliage, green-black, dense, coming up fast. I just had time to note that the pod locator marker was blinking green, meaning that my cargo was down and intact, before my lights went out again.

This time I woke up cold: that was the first datum that registered. The second was that my head hurt; that, and all the rest of me. It took me long enough to write a will leaving everything to the Euthanasia Society to get unstrapped and crack the capsule and crawl out into what the outdoorsy set would have called the bracing mountain air. I tallied my aches and pains, found the bones and joints intact. I ran my suit thermostat up and felt some warmth begin to seep into me.

I was standing on pine needles, if pine needles come in the three-foot length, the diameter of a swizzle stick. They made a springy carpet that covered the ground all around the bases of trees as big as Ionic columns that reached up and up into a deep, green twilight. Far off among the tree trunks I saw the white gleam of snow patches. It was silent, utterly still, with no movement, not even a stir among the wide boughs that spread overhead. My suit instruments told me the air pressure was 16 PSI, oxygen content fifty-one per cent, the ambient temperature minus ten degrees centigrade, all as advertised. The locator dials said the cargo pod was down just over a hundred miles north by east from where I stood. As far as I could tell from the gadgets fitted into my fancy wrist console, everything there was operating normally. And if the information I had gathered was as good as the price said it ought to be, I was within ten miles of where I had planned: half a day's walk from Johnny Thunder's stamping ground. I set my suit controls for minimum power assist, took a compass reading, and started hiking.

9

The low gravity made the going easy, even for a man who had been pounded by a few hundred miles of thin atmosphere; and the suit I was wearing helped, too. You couldn't tell it to look at it, but it had cost somebody the price of a luxury retirement on one of those rhodium-and-glass worlds with taped climate and hot and cold running orgies. In addition to the standard air and temperature controls, and the servo-booster that took the ache out of my walking, it was equipped with every reflex circuit and sense amplifier known to black market science, including a few the League security people would like to get their hands on. The metabolic monitor-and-compensate gear alone was worth the price.

My compass heading took me upslope at a long slant that brought me to the snow line in an hour. Scattered, stunted trees continued for another few thousand feet, ended where the sea-blue glacier began. I got my first look at Vanguard's sky: deep blue, shading down to violet above the ice-crowned peaks that had it all to themselves up here, like a company of kings.

I took a break at the end of the first hour, gave myself a squirt of nutrient syrup and swallowed some water, and listened to eternity passing, silently, one second at a time. I thought about a shipload of colonists, back in the primitive dawn of space travel, setting off into a Universe they knew less about than Columbus did America, adrift for nine years before they crash-landed here. I thought about them stepping out into the great silence of this cold world—men, women, probably children—knowing that there would never, ever, be any returning for them. I thought about them facing that—and going on to live. They'd been tough people, but their kind of toughness had gone out of the world. Now there was only the other kind; my kind. They were pioneer-tough, frontier-tough, full of unfounded hope and determination and big ideas about the future. I was big-city tough, smart-tough, and rat-tough; and the present was enough for me.

"It's the silence," I said aloud. "It gets to you." But the sound of my voice was too small against all that emptiness. I got to my feet and started off toward the next ridge.

Three hours later, the sun was still hanging in the same spot, a dazzle of green above the big top, that every now and then found a hole in the foliage and shot a cold shaft of light down to puddle on the rust-red needles. I had covered almost forty kilometers as the buzzard flies. The spot I was looking for couldn't be far off. I was feeling a little fatigued in spite of the low G, and the sophisticated suit circuitry that took half the load of every muscular contraction, and the stuff the automed was metering into my arm. At that, I was lucky. Back home, I'd have been good for two weeks in a recovery ward after the beating I had taken. I cheered myself with that idea while I leaned against a tree and breathed the enriched canned air the suit had prescribed, and thought positive thoughts to counteract the little lights whirling before my eyes. I was still busy with that when I heard the sound. . . .

Now, it's curious how, after a lifetime surrounded by noises, a few hours without them can change your whole attitude toward air vibrations in the audible range. All I heard was a faint, whooping call, like a lonely sea bird yearning for his mate;

but I came away from the tree as though it had
turned hot, and stood flat-footed, my head cocked,
metering the quality of the sound for clues. It got
louder, which meant closer, with a speed that
suggested the futility of retreat. I looked around
for a convenient sapling to climb, but these pines
were born old; the lowest branch was fifty feet up.
All that was left in the way of concealment was a
few thousand tree trunks. Somehow I had the feeling I'd rather meet whatever it was out in the
open. At least I'd see it as soon as it saw me. I
knew it was something that was alive and ate
meat; a faint, dogmatic voice from my first ances-
tor was telling me that. I did the thing with the
wrist that put the bootleg miniature crater gun in
my palm, and waited while the booming call got
louder and more anguished, like a lovelorn sheep, a
heart-broken bull, a dying elk. I could hear the
thud of big feet now, galloping in a cadence that,
even allowing for the weak gravity field, suggested ponderous size. Then it broke through into
sight, and confirmed great-grandpa's intuition. It
wasn't a hound, or even a hyaenodon, but it was
what a hyaenodon would have been if it had stood
seven feet at the shoulder, had legs as big around
at the ankle as my thigh, a head the size of a one-man
helicab, and jaws that could pick a man up like
Rover trotting home with the evening paper. Maybe
it was that last thought that kept my finger from
tightening on the firing stud. The monster dog
skidded to a halt in a slow-motion flurry of pine
needles, gave a final bellow, and showed me about
a yard of bright red tongue. The rest of him was
brown and black, sleek-furred, loose-hided. His
teeth were big, but not over six inches from gum

line to needle-point. His eyes were shiny black and small, like an elephant's with crescents of red under them. He came on slowly, as if he wanted to get a good look at what he was eating. I could hear his joints creak as he moved. His shoulders were high, bunched with muscle. At each step his foot-wide pads sank into the leaf mould. I felt my knees begin to twitch, while what hackles I had did their best to stand on end. He was ten feet away now, and his breath snorted through nostrils I could have stuck a fist into, like steam around a leaky piston. If he came any closer, I knew my finger would push that stud, ready or not.

"Down, boy!" I said, in what I hoped was a resonant tone of command. He halted, hauled in the tongue, let it out again, then lowered his hind quarters gingerly, like an old lady settling into her favorite rocker. He sat there and looked at me with his head cocked, and I looked back. And while we were doing that, the giant arrived.

11

He came up silently along an aisle among the big trees, and was within fifty feet of me before I saw him, big as he was.

And big he was.

It's easy to talk about a man twelve feet high; that's about twice normal, after all. Just a big man, and let's make a joke about his shoe size.

But twice the height is four times the area of sky he blanks off as he looms over you; eight times the bulk of solid bone and muscle. Sixteen hundred pounds of man, at Earth-normal G. Here he weighed no more than half a ton, but even at that, each leg was holding up five hundred pounds. They were thick, muscle-corded legs that matched the arms and the chest and the neck that was like a section of hundred-year oak supporting the big head. But massive as he was, there was no distortion of proportion. Photographed without a midget in the picture for scale, he would have looked like any other Mr. Universe contender, straight-boned, clean-limbed, every muscle defined, but nothing out of scale. His hair was black, curly, growing in a rough-cut mane, but no rougher than any other man that lives a long way from a barber. He had a close-trimmed beard, thick, black eyebrows over wide-set, pale blue eyes. His skin was weather-burned the color of well-used cowhide. His features were regular enough to be called handsome, if you admire the Jove-Poseidon style. I saw all this as he came striding up to me, dressed in leather, as light on his feet as the dog was heavy. He stopped beside the pooch, patted its head carelessly with a hand the size of first base, looking down at me, and for a ghostly instant I was a child again, looking at the Brobdingnagain world of adults. Thoughts flashed in my mind, phantom images of a world of warmth and love and security and other illusions long forgotten. I pushed those away and remembered that I was Baird Ulrik, professional, out on a job, in a world that had no place for fantasies.

"You're the man they call Johnny Thunder," I said.

He let that pass. Maybe he smiled a little.

"I'm Patton," I told him. "Carl Patton. I bailed out of a ship." I pointed to the sky.

He nodded, "I know," he said. His voice was deep, resonant as a pipe organ; he had a lot of chest for it to bounce around in. "I heard your ship fall." He looked me over, didn't see any compound fractures. "I'm glad you came safely to ground. I hope Woola did not frighten you." His Standard sounded old-fashioned and a little stilted, with a trace of a strange accent. My trained poker face must have slipped a couple of feet at what he said, because he smiled. His teeth were square and porcelain white.

"Why should he?" I said without squeaking. "I've seen my three-year-old niece pat a Great Dane on the knee. That was as high as she could reach."

"Come back with me to my house. I have food, a fire."

I pulled myself together and went into my act: "I've got to get to my cargo pod. There are . . . passengers aboard it."

His face asked questions.

"They're alive—so far," I said. "I have a machine that tells me the pod landed safely, on her chutes. The cannisters are shock-mounted, so if the locator gear survived, so did they. But the equipment might not have. If it was smashed, they'll die."

"This is a strange thing, Carl Patton," he said after I had explained, "to freeze a living man."

"They wouldn't be living long, if they weren't in low-0," I told him. "Third-degree burns over their whole bodies. Probably internals, too. At the med center they can put 'em in viv tanks and regrow their hides. When they wake up, they'll be as good as new." I gave him a significant look, full of do-or-die determination. "If I get there in time, that is. If they come out of it out there . . ." I let the sentence die off without putting words to the kind of death that would be. I made a thing out of looking at the show dials on my wrist. "The pod is down somewhere in that direction." I pointed away up-slope, to the north. "I don't know how far." I shot a look at him to see how that last datum went over. The less I gave away, the better. But he sounded a little more sophisticated than my researches had led me to expect. A slip now could queer everything. "Maybe a hundred miles, maybe more."

He though that one over, looking down at me. His eyes were friendly enough, but in a remote way, like a candle burning in the window of a stranger's house.

"That is bad country, where they have fallen," he said. "The Towers of Nandi are high. You would die on the way there."

I knew it was tough country; I'd picked the spot with care. I gave him my manly, straight-from-the-shoulder look.

"There are ten men out there, my responsibility. I've got to do what I can."

His eyes came back to mine. For the first time, a little fire seemed to flicker alight behind them.

"First you must rest and eat."

I wanted to say more, to set the hook; but just then the world started a slow spin under me. I took a step to catch my balance and a luminous sleet was filling the air, and then the whole thing tilted sideways and I slid off and down into the black place that always waited. . . .

12

I woke up looking at a dancing pattern of orange light on a ceiling of polished red and black wood twenty feet overhead. The light was coming from a fire big enough to roast an ox in, blazing away on a hearth built of rocks the size of tombstones. I was lying on a bed not as large as a handball court, and the air was full of the odor of soup. I crawled to the edge and managed the four-foot jump to the floor. My legs felt like overcooked *pasta*. My ribs ached—probably from a long ride over the giant's shoulder.

He looked across at me from the big table. "You were tired," he said. "And you have many bruises."

I looked down. I was wearing my underwear, nothing else.

"My suit!" I barked, and the words came out

thick, not just from weakness. I was picturing sixty grand worth of equipment and a multi-million credit deal tossed into the reclaimer—or the fire— and a clean set of overalls laid out to replace them.

"There," my host nodded toward the end of the bed. I grabbed, checked. Everything looked OK. But I didn't like it; and I didn't like the idea of being helpless, tended by a man I had business with later.

"You have rested," the big man said. "Now eat."

I sat at the table on a pile of blankets and dipped into a dishpanful of thick broth made of savory red and green vegetables and chunks of tender white meat. There was a bread that was tough and chewy, with a flavor of nuts, and a rough purple wine that went down better than the finest vintage at Arondo's, on Plaisir 4. Afterward, the giant unfolded a chart and pointed to a patch of high relief like coarse-troweled stucco.

"If the pod is there," he said, "it will be difficult. But perhaps it fell here." He indicated a smoother stretch to the south and east of the badlands.

I went through the motions of checking the azimuth on the indicator; the heading I gave him was only about three degrees off true. At 113.8 miles—the position the R&D showed for the pod—we would miss the target by about ten miles.

The big man laid off our line of march on his map. It fell along the edge of what was called the Towers of Nandi.

"Perhaps," he said. He wasn't a man given to wasting words.

"How much daylight is left?" I asked him.

"Fifty hours, a little less." That meant I'd been out for nearly six hours. I didn't like that, either. Time was money, and my schedule was tight.

"Have you talked to anyone?" I looked at the big, not quite modern screen at the side of the room. It was a standard Y-band model with a half-millionth L lag. That meant a four-hour turn-around time to the Ring 8 Station.

"I told the monitor station that you had come safely to ground," he said.

"What else did you tell them?"

"There was nothing more to tell."

I stood. "You can call them again now," I said. "And tell them I'm on my way out to the pod." I gave it the tight-lipped, no-tears-for-me delivery. From the corner of my eye I saw him nod, and for a second I wondered if maybe the famous Ulrik system of analysis had slipped, and this big hunk of virility was going to sit on his haunches and let poor frail little me tackle the trail alone.

"The way will not be easy," he said. "The winds have come to the high passes. Snow lies on the heights of Kooclain."

"My suit heater will handle that part. If you can spare me some food. . . ."

He went to a shelf, lifted down a pack the size and shape of a climate unit for a five-room conapt. I knew then my trap was closing dead on target.

"If my company will not be unwelcome, Carl Patton, I will go with you," he said.

I went through the routine protestations, but in the end I let him convince me. We left half an hour later, after notifying Ring station that we were on the way.

13

Johnny Thunder took the lead, swinging along at an easy amble that covered ground at a deceptive rate, not bothered by the big pack on his back. He was wearing the same leathers he had on when he met me. The only weapon he carried was a ten-foot steel-shod staff. The monster mutt trotted along off-side, nose to the ground; I brought up the rear. My pack was light; the big man pointed out that the less I carried the better time we'd make. I managed to keep up, hanging back a little to make it look good. My bones still ached some, but I was feeling frisky as a colt in the low G. We did a good hour without talking, working up along the angle of a long slope through the big trees. We crested the rise and the big fellow stopped and waited while I came up, puffing a little, but game as they come.

"We will rest here," he said.

"Rest, hell," I came back. "Minutes may make all the difference to those poor devils."

"A man must rest," he said reasonably, and sat down, propping his bare arms on his knees. This put his eyes on a level with mine, standing. I didn't like that, so I sat too.

He took his full ten minutes before starting off again. Johnny Thunder, I saw, was not a man to be bullied. He knew his best pace. Even with all my fancy equipment, I was going to have my hands full walking him to death on his own turf.

That was the plan, just the way they'd laid it out for me, back at Aldo: no wounds on his big corpse when they found it, no dirty work, just a fellow who'd died trying: bigger than your average pictonews hero, but human enough to miscalculate his own giant abilities. Boss would welcome investigation, and he'd check out as clean as a farmhand waiting for the last bus back from the county fair. All I had to do was use my high-tech gear to stay close enough to urge him on. Simple. Not easy, but simple. On that thought I let sleep take me.

14

We crossed a wide valley and headed up into high country. It was cold, and the trees were sparser here, gaunter, dwarfed by the frost and twisted by the winds into hunched shapes that clutched the rock like arthritic hands. There were patches of rotten snow, and a hint in the sky that there might be more to come before long. Not that

I could feel the edge of the wind that came whipping down off the peaks; but the giant was taking it on his bare arms.

"Don't you own a coat?" I asked him at the next stop. We were on a shelf of rock, exposed to the full blast of what was building to a forty-mile gale.

"I have a cape, here." He slapped the pack on his back. "Later I will wear it."

"You make your own clothes?" I was looking at the tanned leather, fur side in, the big sailmaker's stitches.

"A woman made these garments for me," he said. "That was long ago."

"Yeah," I said. I tried to picture him with his woman, to picture how she'd move, what she'd look like. A woman ten feet tall. . . .

"Do you have a picture of her?"

"Only in my heart." He said it matter-of-factly. I wondered how it felt to be the last of your kind, but I didn't ask him that. Instead I asked, "Why do you do it? Live here alone?"

He looked out across a view of refrigerated rock. "This is my home," he said. Another straight answer, with no sho-biz behind it. It just didn't get to this overgrown plowboy. It never occurred to him how he could milk the situation for tears and cash from a few billion sensation-hungry fans. A real-life soap opera. The end of the trail. Poor Johnny Thunder, so brave and so alone.

"Why do *you* do—what you do?" he asked suddenly. I felt my gut clench like a fist.

"What's that supposed to mean?" I got it out between my teeth, while my hand tickled the crater gun out of its wrist clip and into my palm.

"You, too, live alone, Carl Patton. You captain a ship of space. You endure solitude and hardship. And now, you offer your life for your comrades."

"They're not my comrades," I snapped. "They're cash cargo, that's all. No delivery, no payment. And I'm not offering my life. I'm taking a little hike for my health."

He studied me. "Few men would attempt the heights of Kooclain in this season. None without a great reason."

"I've got great reasons; millions of them."

He smiled a faint smile. "You are many things, I think, Carl Patton. But not a fool."

"Let's hit the trail," I said. "We've got a long way to go before I collect."

15

Johnny Thunder held his pace back to what he thought I could manage. The dog seemed a little nervous, raising his nose and snuffling the air, then loping ahead. I easy-footed it after them, with plenty of wheezing on the upslopes and some realistic panting at the breaks, enough to make me look busy, but not enough to give the giant ideas of slowing down. Little by little I upped the cadence in an inobtrusive way, until we were hitting better than four miles per hour. That's a good brisk stride on flat ground at standard G; it would take a trained athlete to keep it up for long. Here, with my suit's efficient piezoelectronic muscles doing most of the work, it was a breeze—for me.

We took a lunch break. The big man dug bread and cheese and a Jeroboam of wine out of his knapsack and handed me enough for two meals. I ate a little of it and tucked the rest into the disposal pocket on my shoulder when he wasn't looking. When he finished his ration—not much bigger than mine—I got to my feet and looked expectant. He didn't move.

"We must rest now for an hour," he told me.

"OK," I said. "You rest alone. I've got a job to do." I started off across the patchy snow and got about ten steps before Bowser gallumphed past me and turned, blocking my route. I started past him on the right and he moved into my path. The same for the left.

"Rest, Carl Patton," Goliath said. He lay back and put his hands under his head and closed his eyes. Well, I couldn't keep him walking, but I could cut into his sleep. I went back and sat beside him.

"Lonely country," I said. He didn't answer.

"Looks like nobody's ever been here before," I added. "Not a beer can in sight." That didn't net a reply either.

"What do you live on in this place?" I asked him. "What do you make the cheese out of, and the bread?"

He opened his eyes. "The heart of the friendly-tree. It is pulverized for flour, or made into a paste and fermented."

"Neat," I said. "I guess you import the wine."

"The fruit of the same tree gives us our wine."
He said 'us' as easily as if he had a wife, six kids,
and a chapter of the Knights of Pythias waiting for
him back home.

"It must have been tough at first," I said. "If
the whole planet is like this, it's hard to see how
your ancestors survived."

"They fought," the giant said, as if that explained everything.

"You don't have to fight anymore," I said.
"You can leave this rock now, live the easy life
somewhere under a sun with a little heat in it."

The giant looked at the sky as if thinking. "We
have a legend of a place where the air is soft and
the soil bursts open to pour forth fruit. I do not
think I would like that land."

"Why not? You think there's some kind of kick
in having things rough?"

He turned his head to look at me. "It is you
who suffer hardship, Carl Patton. I am at home,
whereas you endure cold and fatigue in a place
alien to you."

I grunted. Johnny Thunder had a way of turning
everything I said back at me like a ricochet. "I
heard there was some pretty vicious animal life
here," I said. "I haven't seen any signs of it."

"Soon you will."

"Is that your intuition, or. . . ?"

"A pack of snow scorpions have trailed us for
some hours. When we move out into open ground,
you will see them."

"How do you know?"

"Woola tells me."

I looked at the big hound, sprawled out with his head on his paws. He looked tired.

"How does it happen you have dogs?"

"We have always had dogs."

"Probably had a pair in the original cargo," I said. "Or maybe frozen embryos. I guess they carried breed stock even way back then."

"Woola springs from a line of dogs of war. Her forebear was the mighty courser Standfast, who slew the hounds of King Roon on the Field of the Broken Knife."

"You people fought wars?" He didn't say anything. I snorted. "I'd think as hard as you had to scratch to make a living, you'd have valued your lives too much for that."

"Of what value is a life without truth? King Roon fought for his beliefs. Prince Dahl fought for his own."

"Who won?"

"They fought for twenty hours; and once Prince Dahl fell, and King Roon stood back and bade him rise again. But in the end Dahl broke the back of the King."

"So—did that prove he was right?"

"Little it matters what a man believes, Carl Patton, so long as he believes it with all his heart and soul."

"Nuts. Facts don't care who believes them."

The giant sat up and pointed to the white peaks glistening far away. "The mountains are true," he said. He looked up at the sky, where high, blackish-purple clouds were piled up like battlements. "The sky is true. And these truths are more than the facts of rock and gas."

"I don't understand this poetic talk," I said.

"It's good to eat well, sleep in a good bed, to have the best of everything there is. Anybody that says otherwise is a martyr or a phony."

"What is 'best', Carl Patton? Is there a couch softer than weariness? A better sauce than appetite?"

"You got that out of a book."

"If you crave the easy luxury you speak of, why are you here?"

"That's easy. To earn the money to buy the rest."

"And afterwards—if you do not die on this trek—will you go there, to the pretty world, and eat the fat fruits picked by another hand?"

"Sure," I said. "Why not?" I felt myself sounding mad, and wondered why; and that made me madder than ever. I let it drop and pretended to sleep.

16

Four hours later we topped a long slope and looked out over a thousand square miles of forest and glacier, spread out wide enough to hint at the size of the world called Vangard. We had been walking for nine hours and, lift unit and all, I was beginning to feel it. Big Boy looked as good as new. He shaded his eyes against the sun that was

too small and too bright in a before-the-storm sort
of way, and pointed out along the valley's rim to a
peak a mile or two away.

"There we will sleep," he said.

"It's off our course," I said. "What's wrong
with right here?"

"We need shelter and a fire. Holgrimm will not
grudge us these."

"What's Holgrimm?"

"His lodge stands there."

I felt a little stir along my spine, the way you do
when ghosts come into the conversation. Not that
ghosts worry me; just the people that believe in
them.

We covered the distance in silence. Woola, the
dog, did a lot of sniffing and grunting as we came
up to the lodge. It was built of logs, stripped and
carved and stained red and green and black. There
was a steep gabled roof, slate-tiled, and a pair of
stone chimneys, and a few small windows with
colored glass leaded into them. The big man paused
when we came into the clearing, stood there leaning on his stick and looking around. The place
seemed to be in a good state of preservation. But
then it was built of the same rock and timber as the
country around it. There were no fancy trimmings
to weather away.

"Listen, Carl Patton," the giant said. "Almost,
you can hear Holgrimm's voice here. In a moment,
it seems, he might throw wide the door to welcome us."

"Except he's dead," I said. I went past him and
up to the entrance, which was a slab of black and
purple wood that would have been right in scale on
the front of Notre Dame. I strained two-handed at

the big iron latch, with no luck. Johnny Thunder lifted it with his thumb.

It was cold in the big room. The coating of hard frost on the purple wood floor crunched under our boots. In the deep-colored gloom, I saw stretched animal hides on the high walls, green and red, and gold-furred, brilliant as a Chinese pheasant. There were other trophies: a big, beaked skull three feet long, with a spread of antlers like wings of white ivory, that swept forward to present an array of silver dagger tips, black-ringed. There was a leathery-skinned head that was all jaw and teeth; and a tarnished battle ax, ten feet long, with a complicated head. A long table sat in the center of the room between facing fireplaces as big as city apartments. I saw the wink of light on the big metal goblets, plates, cutlery. There were high-backed chairs around the table; and in the big chair at the far end, facing me, a gray-bearded giant sat with a sword in his hand. The dog whined, a sound that expressed my feelings perfectly.

"Holgrimm awaits us," Johnny's big voice said softly behind me. He went forward, and I broke the paralysis and followed. Closer, I could see the fine frosting of ice that covered the seated giant, glittering in his beard, on the back of his hands, across his open eyes.

Ice rimed the table and the dishes and the smooth, black wood of the chairs. The bared short-sword was frozen to the table. Woola's claws rasped loud on the floor as she slunk behind her master.

"Don't you bury your dead?" I got the words out, a little ragged.

"His women prepared him thus, at his command, when he knew his death was on him."

"Why?"

"That is a secret which Holgrimm keeps well."

"We'd be better off outside," I told him. "This place is like a walk-in freezer."

"A fire will mend that."

"Our friend here will melt. I think I prefer him the way he is."

"Only a little fire, enough to warm our food and make a bed of coals to lie beside."

There was wood in a box beside the door, deep red, hard as granite, already cut to convenient lengths. Convenient for my traveling companion, I mean. He shuffled the eight-foot, eighteen-inch diameter logs as if they were bread sticks. They must have been full of volatile resins, because they lit off on the first match, and burned with a roaring and a smell of mint and camphor. Big Johnny brewed up a mixture of hot wine and some tarry syrup from a pot on the table that he had to break loose from the ice, and handed me a half-gallon pot of the stuff. It was strong, but good, with a taste that was almost turpentine but turned out to be ambrosia instead. There was frozen bread and cheese and a soup he stirred up in the big pot on the hearth. I ate all I could and wasted some more. My large friend gave himself a Spartan ration, raising his mug to our host before he drank.

"How long has he been dead?" I asked.

"Ten of our years." He paused, then added: "That would be over a hundred, League standard."

"Friend of yours?"

"We fought; but later we drank wine together again. Yes, he was my friend."

"How long have you been . . . alone here?"

"Nine years. Holgrimm's house was almost the last the plague touched."

"Why didn't it kill you?"

He shook his head. "The Universe has its jokes, too."

"How was it, when they were all dying?"

The big man cradled his cup in his hands, looking past me into the fire. "At first, no one understood. We had never known disease here, until the first visitors came. Our enemies were the ice wolf and the scorpions, and the avalanche and the killing frost. This was a new thing, the foe we could not see. Some died bewildered, others fled into the forest where their doom caught them at last. Oxandra slew his infant sons and daughters before the choking death could take them. Joshal stood in the snow, swinging his war ax and shouting taunts at the sky until he fell and rose no more."

"What about your family?"

"As you see."

"What?"

"Holgrimm was my father."

The rest of the family, a brother, an uncle, his mother and a few sisters had all gone out alone when the time came, and set off for a spot high up on a peak they called Hel; Johnny didn't know if they'd made it. But I could see it was better that way than burdening the dying survivors with the corpses to dispose of.

Johnny didn't seem to be affected by all this. He just seemed a bit bored.

"Tell me of your own world, Carl Patton," he suggested. "Are all the folk as you, small, but stout of heart for all that?"

I told him I was an exception; most people had sense enough to stay home and enjoy life. He nodded, "Even as I," he said. I pointed out that most folks had a lot more fun than he did, and described the wonders of trideo and electronic golf, and cards and dice and booze. Somehow, I didn't manage to make it sound like much, even to me.

"I would have tools, Carl Patton," he told me. "Such as I have seen in the Great Catalog, for the working of our native stone and woods. This would please me deeply." He looked at his huge hands. "The skill is here, I know it," he said. "To make the beautiful from the raw substance is a great thing, Carl. Do you have such tools at your home?''

I told him I'd built a few model ships as a young fellow, before I'd gotten fully involved in my 'adventurous' life as a free-lance spaceman.

"I finally got my own ship," I explained to him, since he seemed interested. "It was a luxury cruiser, rebuilt from a captured Hukk battlewagon. I kept the armament in place just for the hell of it, but it seemed a lot people got the idea I wouldn't be above using it. I discovered I could trade in and out of some of the toughest hell-ports in the Arm, with no squawks from the Mob. Then, one day, a Navy destroyer hailed me, and boarded and took me in tow. Claimed they'd discovered contraband aboard; then the captain let on maybe there was a way out. Somewhere along then I realized I'd been conned at my own game. The Mob had hijacked the destroyer, and planted the pink stuff on me, and it didn't matter much how it got there; if they sicced the real Navy on me, there I'd be: me and my explanations, but I still had an out. . . ."

"No doubt you defied these miscreants to do their worst, eh, Carl? As any true man would do," he added.

"Not exactly," I told him, wanting to save face for some reason. "I listened to their proposition and let them think I'd play along."

"A dangerous game, Carl," he told me seriously. I shrugged that off and got him to tell me about hunting the ice wolf, which was a native arthropod species: like a man-eating spider, but it supplied furs as fine as any. Hunting warm-blooded tarantu-

las ten feet high wasn't my idea of sport, I told
him. I'd had no sleep for about twenty hours and I
dozed off while he was telling me about the big
fight between the wolves and the scorpions over
the settlement after the snow-patrol broke down.

18

We slept rolled up in the furs Johnny Thunder
took down from the walls and thawed on the hearth.
He was right about the heat. The big blaze melted
the frost in a ten foot semi-circle, but didn't touch
the rest of the room. It was still early afternoon
outside when we hit the trail. I crowded the pace
all I could. After eight hours of it, over increas-
ingly rough ground, climbing all the time, the big
fellow called me on it.

"I'm smaller than you are, but that's no reason
I can't be in shape," I told him. "And I'm used to
higher G. What's the matter, too rough for you?"
I asked the question in an offhand way, but I
listened hard for the answer. So far he looked as
good as new.

"I fare well enough. The trail has been easy."

"The map says it gets rougher fast from here
on."

"The heights will tell on me," he conceded.

"Still, I can go on awhile. But Woola suffers, poor brute."

The dog was stretched out on her side. She looked like a dead horse, if dead horses had tails that wagged when their name was mentioned, and ribs that heaved with the effort of breathing the thin air. Thin by Vangard standards, that is. Oxygen pressure was still over Earth-normal.

"Why not send her back?"

"She would not go. And we will be glad of her company when the snow scorpions come."

"Back to that, eh? You sure you're not imagining them? This place looks as lifeless as a tombstone quarry."

"They wait," he said. "They know me, and Woola. Many times have they tried our alertness—and left their dead on the snow. And so they follow, and wait."

"My gun will handle them." I showed him the legal slug-thrower I carried; he looked it over politely.

"A snow scorpion does not die easily," he said.

"This packs plenty of kick," I said, and demonstrated by blasting a chip off a boulder twenty yards away. The *car-rong!* echoed back and forth among the big trees. He smiled a little.

"Perhaps, Carl Patton."

We slept the night at the timber line.

19

The next day's hike was different, right from the beginning. On the open ground the snow had drifted and frozen into a crust that held my weight, but broke under the giant's feet, and the dog's. There was no kidding about me pushing the pace now. I took the lead and big Johnny had a tough time keeping up. He didn't complain, didn't seem to be breathing too hard; he just kept coming on, stopping every now and then to wait for the pup to catch up, and breaking every hour for a rest.

The country had gotten bleaker as it rose. As long as we'd been among the trees, there had been an illusion of familiarity; not cozy, but at least there was life, almost Earth-type life. You could fool yourself that somewhere over the next rise there might be a house, or a road. But not here. There was just the snow field, as alien as Jupiter, with the long shadows of the western peaks falling across it. And ahead the glacier towering over us against the dark sky, sugar-white in the late sun, deep-sea blue in the shadows.

About the third hour, the big man pointed something out to me, far back along the trail. It looked like a scatter of black pepper against the white.

"The scorpion pack," he said.

I grunted. "We won't outrun them standing here."

"In their own time they will close the gap," he said.

We did nine hours' hike, up one ridge, down the far side, up another, higher one before he called a halt. Dusk was coming on when we made our camp in the lee of an ice buttress, if you can call a couple of hollows in the frozen snow a camp. The big man got a small fire going, and boiled some soup. He gave me my usual hearty serving, but it seemed to me he shorted himself and the dog a little.

"How are the supplies holding out?" I asked him.

"Well enough," was all he said.

The temperature was down to minus nine centigrade now. He unpacked his cloak, a black and orange striped super-sheepskin the size of a mains'l, and wrapped himself up in it. He and the dog slept together, curled for warmth. I turned down the invitation to join them.

"My circulation's good," I said. "Don't worry about me."

But in spite of the suit, I woke up shivering, and had to set the thermostat a few notches higher. Big Boy didn't seem to mind the cold. But then, an animal his size had an advantage. He had less radiating surface per unit weight. It wasn't freezing that would get him—not unless things got a lot worse.

When he woke me, it was deep twilight; the sun was gone behind the peaks to the west. The route

ahead led up the side of a thirty-degree snow
slope. There were enough outcroppings of rock
and tumbled ice blocks to make progress possible,
but it was slow going. The pack on our trail had
closed the gap while we slept; I estimated they
were ten miles behind now. There were about
twenty-five of the things, strung out in a wide
crescent. I didn't like that; it suggested more intelligence than anything that looked as bad as the
pictures I'd seen. Woola rolled her eyes and showed
her teeth and whined, looking back at them. The
giant just kept moving forward, slow and steady.

"How about it?" I asked him at the next break.
"Do we just let them pick the spot? Or do we fort
up somewhere, where they can only jump us from
about three and a half sides?"

"They must come to us."

I looked back down the slope we had been
climbing steadily for more hours than I could keep
track of, trying to judge their distance.

"Not more than five miles," I said. "They
could have closed any time in the last couple of
hours. What are they waiting for?"

He glanced up at the high ridge, dazzling two
miles above. "Up there, the air is thin and cold.
They sense that we will weaken."

"And they're right."

"They too will be weakened, Carl Patton, though
not perhaps so much as we." He said this as
unconcernedly as if he were talking about whether
tomorrow would be a good day for a picnic.

"Don't you care?" I asked him. "Doesn't it
matter to you if a pack of hungry meat-eaters
corners you in the open?"

"It is their nature," he said simply.

"A stiff upper lip is nifty—but don't let it go to your head. How about setting up an ambush—up there?" I pointed out a jumble of rock slabs a hundred yards above.

"They will not enter it."

"OK," I said. "You're the wily native guide. I'm just a tourist. We'll play it your way. But what do we do when it gets dark?"

"The moon will soon rise."

In the next two hours we covered about three-quarters of a mile. The slope was close to forty-five degrees now. Powdery snow went cascading down in slow plumes with every step. Without the suit I don't know if I could have stayed with it, even with the low gravity. Big Johnny was using his hands a lot now; and the dog's puffing was piteous to hear.

"How old is the mutt?" I asked when we were lying on our backs at the next break, with my trailmates working hard to get some nourishment out of what to them was some very thin atmosphere, and me faking the same distress, while I breathed the rich mixture from my suit collector.

"Three years."

"That would be about thirty-five Standard. How long . . ." I remembered my panting and did some, ". . . do they live?"

"No one . . . knows."

"What does that mean?"

"Her kind . . . die in battle."

"It looks like she'll get her chance."

"For that . . . she is grateful."

"She looks scared to death," I said. "And dead beat."

"Weary, yes. But fear is not bred in her."

We made another half mile before the pack decided the time had come to move in to the attack.

20

The dog knew it first; she gave a bellow like a gut-shot elephant and took a twenty-foot bound down-slope to take up her stand between us and them. It couldn't have been a worse position from the defensive viewpoint, with the exception of the single factor of our holding the high ground. It was a featureless stretch of frozen snow, tilted on edge, naked as a tin roof. The big fellow used his number forty's to stamp out a hollow, working in a circle to widen it.

"You damn fool, you ought to be building a mound," I yelled at him. "That's a cold grave you're digging."

"Do as I do . . . Carl Patton," he panted. "For your life."

"Thanks; I'll stay topside." I picked a spot off to his left and kicked some ice chunks into a heap to give me a firing platform. I made a big show of checking the slug-thrower, then inobtrusively set the crater gun for max range, narrow beam. I don't

know why I bothered playing it foxy; Big Boy
didn't know the difference between a legal weapon
and contraband. Maybe it was just the instinct to
have an ace up the sleeve. By the time I finished,
the pack was a quarter of a mile away and coming
up fast, not running or leaping, but twinkling along
on clusters of steel-rod legs that ate up the ground
like a fire eats dry grass.

"Carl Patton, it would be well if you stood by
my back," the big man called.

"I don't need to hide behind you," I barked.

"Listen well!" he said, and for the first time his
voice lacked the easy, almost idle tone. "They
cannot attack in full charge. First must they halt
and raise their barb. In that moment are they
vulnerable. Strike for the eye—but beware the
ripping claws!"

"I'll work at a little longer range," I called
back, and fired a slug at one a little in advance of
the line but still a couple of hundred yards out.
There was a bright flash against the ice; a near
miss. The next one was dead on—a solid hit in the
center of the leaf-shaped plate of tarnish-black
armor that covered the thorax. He didn't even
break stride.

"Strike for the eye, Carl Patton!"

"What eye?" I yelled. "All I see is plate armor
and pistons!" I fired for the legs, missed, missed
again, then sent fragments of a limb flying. The
owner may have faltered for a couple of micro-
seconds, or maybe I just blinked. I wasn't even
sure which one I had hit. They came on, closing
ranks now, looking suddenly bigger, more deadly,
like an assault wave of light armor, barbed and
spiked and invulnerable, with nothing to stop them

but a man with a stick, a worn-out old hound, and me, with my popgun. I felt the weapon bucking in my hand, and realized I had been firing steadily. I took a step back, dropped the slug thrower, and palmed the crater gun as the line reached the spot where Woola crouched, waiting.

But instead of slamming into the big dog at full bore, the pair facing her skidded to a dead stop, executed a swift but complicated rearrangement of limbs, dropping their forward ends to the ground, bringing their hindquarters up and over, unsheathing two-foot-long stingers that poised, ready to plunge down into the unprotected body of the animal. . . .

I wouldn't have believed anything so big could move so fast. She came up from her flattened position like a cricket off a hot plate, was in mid-air, twisting to snap down at the thing on the left with jaws like a bear trap, landed sprawling, spun, leaped, snapped, and was poised, snarling, while two ruined attackers flopped and stabbed their hooks into the ice before her. I saw all this in a fast half-second while I was bringing the power gun up, squeezing the firing stud to pump a multi-megawatt jolt into the thing that was rearing up in front of me. The shock blasted a foot-wide pit in it, knocked it a yard backward—but didn't slow its strike. The barb whipped up, over, and down to bury itself in the ice between my feet.

"The eye!" The big man's voice boomed at me over the snarls of Woola and the angry buzzing that was coming from the attackers. "The eye, Carl Patton!"

I saw it then: a three-inch patch like reticulated glass, deep red, set in the curve of armor above

the hook-lined prow. It exploded as I fired. I
swiveled left and fired again, from the corner of
my eye saw the big man swing his club left, right.
I was down off my mound, working my way over
to him, slamming shots into whatever was closest.
The scorpions were all around us, but only half a
dozen at a time could crowd in close to the edge of
the twelve-foot depression the giant had tramped
out. One went over, pushed from behind, scrabbling for footing, and died as the club smashed
down on him. I killed another and jumped down
beside the giant.

"Back to back, Carl Patton," he called. A pair
came up together over a barricade of dead monsters,
and while they teetered for attack position I shot
them, then shot the one that mounted their thresh-
ing corpses. Then suddenly the pressure slackened,
and I was hearing the big man's steam-engine
puffing, the dog's rasping snarls, was aware of a
pain in my thigh, of the breath burning in my
throat. A scorpion jittered on his thin legs ten feet
away, but he came no closer. The others were
moving back, buzzing and clacking. I started up
over the side and an arm like a jib boom stopped
me.

"They must . . . come to us." the giant wheezed
out the words. His face was pink and he was
having trouble getting enough air, but he was
smiling.

"If you say so," I said.

"Your small weapon strikes a man's blow," he
said, instead of commenting on my stupidity.

"What are they made of? They took my rounds
like two-inch flint steel."

"They are no easy adversaries," he said. "Yet

we killed nine." He looked across at where the dog stood panting, facing the enemy. "Woola slew five. They learn caution—" He broke off, looking down at me, at my leg. He went to one knee, touched a tear in my suit I hadn't noticed. That shook me, seeing the ripped edge of the material. Not even a needler could penetrate the stuff—but one of those barbs had.

"The hide is unbroken," he said. "Luck was with you this day, Carl Patton. The touch of the barb is death."

Something moved behind him and I yelled and fired and a scorpion came plunging down on the spot where he'd been standing an instant before. I fell and rolled, came around, put one in the eye just as Johnny Thunder's club slammed home in the same spot. I got to my feet and the rest of them were moving off, back down the slope.

"You damned fool!" I yelled at the giant. Rage broke my voice. "Why don't you watch yourself?"

"I am in your debt, Carl Patton," was all he said.

"Debt, hell! Nobody owes me anything—and that goes both ways!"

He didn't answer that, just looked down at me, smiling a little, like you would at an excited child. I took a couple of deep breaths of warmed and fortified tank air and felt better—but not much.

"Will you tell me your true name, small warrior?" the giant said.

I felt ice form in my chest.

"What do you mean?" I stalled.

"We have fought side by side.. It is fitting that we exchange the secret names our mothers gave us at birth."

"Oh, magic, eh? Juju. The secret word of power. Skip it, big fellow. Johnny Thunder is good enough for me."

"As you will . . . Carl Patton." He went to see to the dog then, and I checked to see how badly my suit was damaged. There was a partial power loss in the leg servos and the heat was affected, too. That wasn't good. There were still a lot of miles to walk out of the giant before the job was done.

When we hit the trail half an hour later I was still wondering why I had moved so fast to save the life of the man I'd come here to kill.

21

We halted for sleep three hours later. It was almost full dark when we turned in, curled up in pits trampled in the snow. Johnny Thunder said the scorpions wouldn't be back until they'd eaten their dead, but I sweated inside my insulated longjohns as the last of the light faded to a pitch black like the inside of an unmarked grave. Then I must have dozed off, because I woke with blue-white light in my face. The inner moon, Cronus, had risen over the ridge, a cratered disk ten degrees wide, almost full, looking close enough to jump up and bang my head on, if I'd felt like jumping. I didn't.

We made good time in the moonlight, considering the slope of the glacier's skirt we were climbing. At forty-five thousand feet, we topped the barrier and looked down the far side and across a shadowed valley to the next ridge, twenty miles away, silver-white against the stars.

"Perhaps on the other side we will find them," the giant said. His voice had lost some of its timbre. His face looked frostbitten, pounded numb by the sub-zero wind. Woola crouched behind him, looking shrunken and old.

"Sure," I said. "Or maybe beyond the next one, or the one after that."

"Beyond these ridges lie the Towers of Nandi. If your friends have fallen there, their sleep will be long—and ours as well."

It was two marches to the next ridge. By then the moon was high enough to illuminate the whole panorama from the crest. There was nothing in sight but ice. We camped in the lee of the crest, then went on. The suit was giving me trouble, unbalanced as it was, and the toes of my right foot were feeling the frost.

Sometime, about mid-afternoon, I noticed we'd veered off our route as if to skirt a mesa-like rock formation ahead. I registered a gripe about the extra mileage and proposed to get back to the direct route.

"Go if you will, Carl Patton. Perhaps I have not been fair to you, thus to indulge my personal taboo."

"What's that supposed to mean?" I yelled at

him. I was too beat to be diplomatic. He ignored
the bad manners and turned to look at the mesa.

"Yonder rises Hel," he said. "I would prefer
not to know the fate of my sisters and their young."

I did a 'shucks, fella, I didn't mean . . .' number,
and we went on, following his detour. An hour or
two later, Woola, scouting ahead, halted and began skirting something that looked like a low mound
of snow. Then she whined and her ears and tail
drooped. She turned and came back to put up a
paw for Johnny Thunder to take while he patted
the big shaggy head. He went forward to look at
what she'd found and I trailed along, wondering
what it was that could make the old war-dog wilt
like a whipped puppy. The giant had knelt to brush
away snow, and when I came around him I saw
the face, as beautiful as any ancient image of a
love goddess, and on the same heroic scale; a
young face, almost smiling, with a lock of red-
gold hair across the noble ice-pale forehead. All of
a sudden I was all out of wisecracks. Here was a
beauty that wars could have been fought over,
dead and frozen these hundred years. Too bad I
didn't have the magic spell that would waken her.

"Adainn was the youngest," the giant said.
"Only a girl, barely of marriageable age. Now she
is the bride of the ice, lying in his cold embrace."

"Good looking dolly," I said, and all of a
sudden I felt a sense of loss that almost blacked
me out. I heard myself saying "No, no! NO!" and
struggling against Johnny's big arm, barring my
way, while Woola rose from her haunches, and
took a position standing protectively over the corpse.
After a while I was sitting in the snow, with water

running out of my eyes and freezing, and big Johnny saying:

"Be none ashamed, Carl. Any man must love her when he sees her, be he large or small."

I told him he was nuts, and got up and arranged my load, not looking at her somehow, for some reason, and then Johnny covered her face again, and said, "Fare thee well, my little sister. Now we must tend the living," and we went on. Johnny was more silent than usual all day, and in spite of the hot concentrates I sucked on the sly as I hiked, and the synthetic pep the hypospray metered into an artery, I was starting to feel it now. But not as badly as Big Johnny. He had a gaunt, starved look, and he hiked as though he had anvils tied to his feet. He was still feeding himself and the dog meager rations, and forcing an equal share on me. When he wasn't looking I stuffed what I couldn't eat in the disposal and watched him starve. But he was tough; he starved slowly, grudgingly, fighting for every inch.

He never complained. He could have gotten up and started back any time, with no apologies. He'd already made a better try than anyone could expect, even of a giant. As for me, all I had to do was picture that fat bank account, and all the big juicy steaks and big soft beds with beautiful women in them and the hand-tooled cars and the penthouse with a view all that cash was going to buy for me. As long as I kept my mind on that, the pain seemed remote and unimportant. Baird Ulrik could take it, all right. And after all, Big Boy was only human, like Woola and me, and as long as he could get up and go on one more time, so could I: I almost felt sorry for the big mutt, who went on just because she couldn't imagine anything else to do, much less a fancy doghouse with plenty of bones but I stifled that. It was no time to be sentimental. At least, Big Johnny was no longer asking me those strangely embarassing questions of his. The big dope couldn't even imagine treachery and betrayal. And to hell with that, too.

That night, lying back of a barrier he'd built up out of snow blocks against the wind, he asked me a question.

"What is it like, Carl Patton, to travel across the space between the worlds?"

"Solitary confinement," I told him.

"You do not love your solitude?"

"What does that matter? I do my job."

"What do you love, Carl Patton?"

"Wine, women, and song," I said. "And you can even skip the song, in a pinch."

"A woman waits for you?"

"Women," I corrected. "But they're not waiting."

"Your loves seem few, Carl Patton. What then do you hate?"

"Fools," I said.

"Is it fools who have driven you here?"

"Me? Nobody drives me anywhere. I go where I like."

"Then it is freedom you strive for. Have you found it here on my world, Carl Patton?" His face was a gaunt mask like a weathered carving, but his voice was laughing at me.

"You know you're going to die out here, don't you?" I hadn't intended to say that. But I did; and my tone was savage to my own ears.

He looked at me, the way he always did before

he spoke, as if he were trying to read a message written on my face.

"A man must die," he said.

"You don't have to be here," I said. "You could break it off now, go back, forget the whole thing."

"As could you, Carl Patton."

"Me quit?" I snapped. "No thanks. My job's not done."

He nodded. "A man must do what he sets out to do. Else is he no more than a snowflake driven before the wind."

"You think this is a game?" I barked. "A contest? Do or die, or maybe both, and may the best man win?"

"With whom would I contest, Carl Patton? Are we not comrades of the trail?"

"We're strangers," I said. "You don't know me and I don't know you. And you can skip trying to figure out my reasons for what I do."

"You set out to save the lives of the helpless, because it was your duty."

"It's not yours! You don't have to break yourself on these mountains! You can leave this ice factory, live the rest of your days as a hero of the masses, have everything you'd ever want—"

"What I want, no *man* can give me."

"I suppose you hate us," I said. "The strangers that came here and brought a disease that killed your world."

"Who can hate a natural force?"

"All right—what *do* you hate?"

For a minute I thought he wasn't going to answer. "I hate the coward within me," he said. "The voice that whispers counsels of surrender. But if I

fled, and saved this flesh, what spirit would then
live on to light it?''

"You want to run—then run!" I almost yelled.
"You're going to lose this race, big man! Quit
while you can!"

"I will go on—while I can. If I am lucky, the
flesh will die before the spirit."

"Spirit, hell! You're a suicidal maniac!"

"Then am I in good company, Carl Patton."

I let him take that one.

22

We passed the hundred-mile mark the next march.
We crossed another ridge, higher than the last.
The cold was sub-artic, the wind a flaying knife.
The moon set, and after a couple of eternities,
dawn came. My locator told me when we passed
within ten miles of the pod. All its systems were
still going. The power cells were good for a hundred years. If I slipped up at my end, the frozen
miners might wake up to a new century; but they'd
wake up.

Johnny Thunder was a pitiful sight now. His
hands were split and bloody, his hollow cheeks
and bloodless lips cracked and peeling from
frostbite, the hide stretched tight over his bones.

He moved slowly, heavily, wrapped in his furs. But he moved. I ranged out ahead, keeping the pressure on. The dog was in even worse shape than his master. She trailed far behind on the up-slopes, spent most of each break catching up. Little by little, in spite of my heckling, the breaks got longer, the marches shorter. The big man knew how to pace himself, in spite of my gadfly presence. He meant to hang on, and make it. So much for my plans. It was late afternoon again when we reached the high pass that the big man said led into the badlands he called the Towers of Nandi. I came up the last stretch of trail between sheer ice walls and looked out over a vista of ice peaks sharp as broken bottles, packed together like shark's teeth, rising up and up in successive ranks that reached as far as the eye could see.

I turned to urge the giant to waste some more strength hurrying to close the gap, but he beat me to it. He was pointing, shouting something I couldn't hear for a low rumble that had started up. I looked up, and the whole side of the mountain was coming down at me.

23

The floor was cold. It was the tiled floor of the crech locker room, and I was ten years old, and lying on my face, held there by the weight of a kid called Soup, age fourteen, with the physique of an ape and and IQ to match.

When he'd first pushed me back against the wall, knocked aside my punches, and thrown me to the floor, I had cried, called for help to the ring of eager-eyed spectators, most of whom had more than once felt the weight of Soup's knobby knuckles. None of them moved. When he'd bounced my head on the floor and called to me to say uncle, I opened my mouth to say it, and then spat in his face instead. What little restraint Soup had left him then. Now his red-bristled forearm was locked under my jaw, and his knee was in the small of my back, and I knew, without a shadow of a doubt, that Soup was a boy who didn't know his own strength, who would stretch his growing muscles with all the force he could muster—caught up and carried away in the thrill of the discovery of his own animal power—would bend my back until my spine snapped, and I'd be dead, dead, dead forevermore, at the hands of a moron.

Unless I saved myself. I was smarter than Soup—smarter than any of them. Man had conquered the animals with his mind—and Soup was an animal. He couldn't—couldn't kill me. Not if I used my brain, instead of wasting my strength against an animal body twice the size of my own.

I stepped outside my body and looked at myself, saw how he knelt on me, gripping his own wrist, balancing with one outflung foot. I saw how, by twisting to my right side, I could slide out from under the knee; and then, with a sudden movement . . .

His knee slipped off-center as I moved under him. With all the power in me, I drew up, doubling my body; unbalanced, he started to topple to his right, still gripping me. I threw myself back against him, which brought my head under his chin. I reached back, took a double handful of coarse red hair, and ripped with all my strength.

He screamed, and his grip was gone. I twisted like an eel as he grabbed for my hands, still tangled in his hair; I lunged and buried my teeth in his thick ear. He howled and tried to tear away, and I felt the cartilage break, tasted salty blood. He ripped my hands away, taking hair and a patch of scalp with them. I saw his face, contorted like a demon-mask as he sprawled away from me, still grasping my wrists. I brought my knee up into his crotch, and saw his face turn to green clay. I jumped to my feet; he writhed, coiled, making an ugly choking sound. I took aim and kicked him hard in the mouth. I landed two more carefully placed kicks, with my full weight behind them, before the rudimentary judgement of the audience awoke and they pulled me away. . . .

There was movement near me. I heard the rasp

of something hard and rough against another hardness. Light appeared. I drew a breath, and saw the white-bearded face of an ancient man looking down at me from far above, from the top of a deep well. . . .

"You still live, Carl Patton." The giant's voice seemed to echo from a long way off. I saw his big hands come down, straining at a quarter-ton slab of ice, saw him lift it slowly, toss it aside. There was snow in his hair, ice droplets in his beard. His breath was frost.

"Get out of here." I forced the words out past the broken glass in my chest. "Before the rest comes down."

He didn't answer; he lifted another slab, and my arms were free. I tried to help, but that just made more snow spill down around my shoulders. He put his big impossible hands under my arms and lifted, dragged me up and out of my grave. I lay on my back and he sprawled beside me. The dog Woola crawled up to him, making anxious noises. Little streamers of snow were coming down from above, being whipped away by the wind. A mass of ice the size of a carrier tender hung cantilevered a few hundred feet above.

"Run, you damned fool!" I yelled. It came out as a whisper. He got to his knees, slowly. He scooped me up, rose to his feet. Ice fragments clattered down from above. He took a step forward, toward the badlands.

"Go back," I managed. "You'll be trapped on the far side!"

He halted, as more ice rattled down. "Alone, Carl Patton . . . would *you* turn back?"

"No," I said. "But there's no reason . . . now . . . for you to die. . . ."

"Then we will go on." He took another step, and staggered as a pebble of ice the size of a basketball struck him a glancing blow on the shoulder. The dog snarled at his side. It was coming down around us like rice at a wedding now. He went on, staggering like a drunk, climbing up over the final drift. There was a boom like a cannon-shot from above; air whistled past us, moving out. He made three more paces and went down, dropped me, knelt over me like a shaggy tent. I heard him grunt as the ice fragments struck him. Somewhere behind us there was a smash like a breaking dam. The air was full of snow, blinding, choking. The light faded. . . .

24

The dead were crying. It was a sad, lost sound, full of mournful surprise that life had been so short and so full of mistakes. I understood how they felt. Why shouldn't I? I was one of them.

But corpses didn't have headaches, as well as I could remember. Or cold feet, or weights that crushed them against sharp rocks. Not unless the stories about where the bad ones went were true. I

opened my eyes to take a look at Hell, and saw the
hound. She whined again, and I got my head
around and saw an arm bigger than my leg. The
weight I felt was what was left of Johnny Thunder,
sprawled across me, under a blanket of broken ice.

It took me half an hour to work my way free.
The suit was what had saved me, of course, with
its automatic defensive armor. I was bruised, and a
rib or two were broken, but there was nothing I
couldn't live with until I got back to base and my
six million credits.

Because the job was done. The giant didn't
move while I was digging out, didn't stir when I
thumbed up his eyelid. He still had some pulse,
but it wouldn't last long. He had been bleeding
from the ice wounds on his face and hands, but the
blood had frozen. What the pounding hadn't
finished, the cold would. And even if he came
around, the wall of ice behind him closed the pass
like a vault door. When the sob sisters arrived to
check on their oversized pet they'd find him here,
just as I would describe him, the noble victim of
the weather and the piece of bad luck that had
made us miss our target by a tragic ten miles, after
that long, long hike. They'd have a good syndi-
cated cry over how he'd given his all, and then
close the book on another footnote to history. It
had worked out just the way I'd planned. Not that
I got any big kick out of my cleverness once
again. It was routine, just a matter of analyzing the
data.

"So long, Johnny Thunder," I said. "You were
a lot of man."

The dog lifted her head and whined. I made
soothing sounds and switched the lift-unit built

into my suit to maximum assist and headed for the pod, fifteen miles away, in *that* direction. I heard Woola's tail flopping as she wagged goodbye. Too bad; but there was no way I could help a mutt as big as a shire horse.

25

The twenty-foot-long cargo unit was nestled in a drift of hard-packed snow, in a little hollow among barren rock peaks, not showing a scratch. I wasn't surprised; the auto gear I had installed could have soft-landed a china shop without cracking a teacup. I had contracted to deliver my load intact, and it was a point of pride with me to fulfill the letter of a deal. I was so busy congratulating myself on that that I was fifty feet from it before I noticed that the snow had been disturbed around the pod: trampled, maybe, then brushed out to conceal the tracks. By then it was too late to become invisible; if there was anybody around, he had already seen me. I stopped ten feet from the entry hatch and went through the motions of collapsing in a pitiful little heap, all tuckered out from my exertions, meanwhile looking around, over, and under the pod. I didn't see anything.

I lay where I was long enough for anybody who

wanted to to make his entrance. No takers. That left the play up to me. I made a production out of getting my feet under me and staggering to the entry hatch. The scratches there told me that part of the story. The port mechanism was still intact. It opened on command and I crawled into the lock. Inside, everything looked normal. The icebox seal was tight, the dials said the cooler units were operating perfectly, not that they had a whole lot to do in this natural freezer of a world. I almost let it go at that, but not quite. I don't know why, except that a lifetime of painful lessons had taught me to take nothing for granted. It took me half an hour to get the covers off the reefer controls. When I did, I saw it right away: a solenoid hung in the half-open position. It was the kind of minor malfunction you might expect after a hard landing— but not if you knew what I knew. It had been jimmied, the support bent a fractional millimeter out of line, just enough to jam the action—and incidentally to actuate the heating cycle that would thaw the ten men inside the cold room in ten hours flat. I freed it, heard gas hiss into the lines, then cracked the vault door and checked visually. The inside gauge read $+3°$ absolute. The temperature hadn't had time to start rising yet; the ten long boxes and their contents were still intact. That meant the tampering had been done recently. I was still mulling over the implications of that deduction when I heard the crunch of feet on the ice outside the open lock.

26

Illini looked older than he had when I had seen him last, back in the plush bureaucratic setting of League Central. His monkey face behind the cold mask looked pinched and bloodless; his long nose was pink with cold, his jaw a scruffy, unshaven blue. He didn't seem surprised to see me. He stepped up through the hatch and a second man followed him. They looked around. Their glance took in the marks in the frost crust around the reefer, and held on the open panel.

"Everything all right here?" the little man asked me. He made it casual, as if we'd just happened to meet on the street.

"Almost," I said. "A little trouble with a solenoid. Nothing serious."

Illini nodded as if that was par for the course. His eyes flickered over me. "Outside, you seemed to be in difficulty," he said. "I see you've made a quick recovery."

"It must have been psychosomatic," I said. "Getting inside took my mind off it."

"I take it the subject is dead?"

"Hell, no," I said. "He's alive and well in

Phoenix, Arizona. How did you find the pod, Illini?''

"I was lucky enough to persuade the black marketeer who supplied your homing equipment to sell me its twin, tuned to the same code.'' He looked mildly amused. "Don't be too distressed, Ulrik. There are very few secrets from an unlimited budget.''

"One is enough,'' I said, "played right. But you haven't said why.''

"The scheme you worked out was clever,'' he said. "Somewhat over-devious, perhaps—but clever. Up to a point. It was apparent from the special equipment installed in the pod that you had some idea of your cargo surviving the affair.''

"So?''

"You wanted to present the public with a tidy image to treasure, Ulrik. Well and good. But the death of a freak in a misguided attempt to rescue men who were never in danger would smack of the comic. People might be dissatisfied. They might begin investigating the circumstances which allowed their pet to waste himself. But if it appears he *might* have saved the men—then the public will accept his martyrdom.''

"You plan to spend ten men on the strength of that theory?''

"It's a trivial price to pay for extra insurance.''

"And here you are, to correct my mistakes. How do you plan to square it with the Monitor Service? They take a dim view of unauthorized planetfalls.''

Illini gave me his I-just-ate-the-canary look. "I'm here quite legally. By great good fortune, my yacht happened to be cruising in the vicinity and picked up your U-beam. Ring Station accepted my offer of assistance.''

''I see. And what have you got in mind for me?''

''Just what was agreed on, of course. I have no intention of complicating the situation at this point. We'll proceed with the plan precisely as conceived— with the single exception I've noted. I can rely on your discretion, for obvious reasons. Your fee is already on deposit at Credit Central.''

''You've got it all worked out, haven't you?'' I said, trying to sound sarcastic. ''But you overlooked one thing: I'm temperamental. I don't like people making changes in my plans.''

Illini lifted a lip. ''I'm aware of your penchant for salving your conscience as a professional assassin by your nicety in other matters. But in this case I'm afraid *my* desires must prevail.'' The hand of the man behind him strayed casually to the gun at his hip. So far, he hadn't said a word. He didn't have to. He'd be a good man with a sidearm. Illini wouldn't have brought anything but the best. Or maybe the second best. It was a point I'd probably have to check soon.

''Our work here will require only a few hours,'' Illini said. ''After that . . .'' he made an expansive gesture. ''We're all free to take up other matters.'' He smiled as though everything had been cleared up. ''By the way, where is the body? I'll want to view it, just as a matter of routine.''

I folded my arms and leaned against the bulkhead. I did it carefully, just in case I was wrong about a few things. ''What if I don't feel like telling you?'' I asked him.

"In that case, I'd be forced to insist." Illini's eyes were wary. The gunsel had tensed.

"Uh-uh," I said. "This is a delicate setup. A charred corpse wouldn't help the picture."

"Podnac's instructions are to disable, not to kill."

"For a hired hand, you seem to be taking a lot of chances, Illini. It wouldn't do for the public to get the idea that the selfless motive of eliminating a technicality so that progress could come to Vangard, as the Boss told it, is marred by some private consideration."

Illini lifted his shoulders. "We own an interest in the planetary exploitation contract, yes. Someone was bound to profit. Why not those who made it possible?"

"That's another one on me," I said. "I should have held out for a percentage."

"That's enough gossip," Illini said. "Don't try to stall me, Ulrik. Speak up or suffer the consequences."

I shook my head. "I'm calling your bluff, Illini. The whole thing is balanced on a knife's edge. Any sign of trouble here—even a grease spot on the deck—and the whole thing is blown."

Podnac made a quick move and his gun was in his hand. I grinned at it. "That's supposed to scare me so I go outside where you can work a little better, eh?"

"I'm warning you, Ulrik—"

"Skip it. I'm not going anywhere. But you're leaving, Illini. You've got your boat parked somewhere near here. Get in it and lift off. I'll take it from there."

"You fool! You'd risk the entire operation for the sake of a piece of mawkish sentiment?"

"It's my operation, Illini. I'll play it out my way or not at all. I'm like that. That's why you hired me, remember?"

He drew a breath like a man getting ready for a deep dive, snorted it out. "You don't have a chance, Ulrik! You're throwing everything away—for what?"

"Not quite everything. You'll still pay off for a finished job. It's up to you. You can report you checked the pod and found everything normal. Try anything else and the bubble pops."

"There are two of us. We could take you bare-handed."

"Not while I've got my hand on the gun under my arm."

The little man's eyes ate me raw. There were things he wanted to say, but instead he made a face like a man chewing glass and jerked his head at his hired hand. They walked sideways to the hatch and jumped down. I watched them back away.

"I'll get you for this," Illini told me when he finally decided I was bluffing. "I promise you that," he added.

"No, you won't," I said. "You'll just count those millions and keep your mouth shut. That's the way the Boss would like it."

They turned and I straightened and dropped my hands. Podnac spun and fired and the impact knocked me backward twenty feet across the hold.

The world was full of roaring lights and blazing sounds, but I held onto a slender thread of consciousness, built it into a rope, crawled back up it. I did it because I had to. I made it just in time. Podnac was coming through the hatch, Illini's voice yapping behind him. I covered him and pressed the stud and blew him back out of sight.

27

I was numb all over, like a thumb that's just been hit by a hammer. I felt hot fluid trickling down the inside of my suit, felt broken bones grate. I tried to move and almost blacked out. I knew then: this was one scrape I wouldn't get out of. I'd had it. Illini had won.

His voice jarred me out of a daze.

"He fired against my order, Ulrik! You heard me tell him! I'm not responsible!"

I blinked a few times and could see the little man through the open port, standing in a half crouch on the spot where I'd last seen him, watching the dark hatchway for the flash that would finish him. He was holding the winning cards, and didn't know it. He didn't know how hard I'd been hit, that he could have strolled in and finished the job with no opposition. He thought tough, smart Baird Ulrik had rolled with another punch, was holding on him now, cool and deadly and in charge of everything.

OK. I'd do my best to keep him thinking that. I was done for, but so was he—if I could con him into leaving now. When the Monitors showed up and found my corpse and the note I'd manage to write before the final night closed down, Illini and Company would be out of the planet-stealing business and into a penal colony before you could say malfeasance in high office. I looked around for my voice, breathed on it a little, and called:

"We won't count that one, Illini. Take your boy and lift off. I'll be watching. So will the Monitor scopes. If you try to land again you'll have them to explain to."

"I'll do as you say, Ulrik. It's your show. I . . . I'll have to use a lift harness on Podnac."

I didn't answer that one. I couldn't. That worried Illini.

"Ulrik? I'm going to report that I found everything in order. Don't do anything foolish. Remember your six million credits."

"Get going," I managed. I watched him back up a few steps, then turn and scramble up the slope. The lights kept fading and coming up again.

Quite suddenly Illini was there again, guiding the slack body of his protégé as it hung in the harness. When I looked again they were gone. Then I let go of whatever it was I had been hanging onto, and fell forever through endlessness.

When I woke up, Johnny Thunder was sitting beside me.

28

He gave me water. I drank it and said, "You big, dumb ox! What are you doing here?" I said that, but all that came out was a dry wheeze, like a collapsing lung. I lay with my head propped against the wall, the way he had laid me out, and looked at the big, gaunt face, the cracked and peeling lips, the matted hair caked with ice, the bright blue eyes fixed on mine.

"I woke and found you had gone, Carl Patton." His voice had lost its resonance. He sounded like an old man. "Woola led me here."

I thought that over—and then I saw it. It almost made me grin. A note written in blood might poke a hole in Illini's plans—but a live giant would sink them with all hands.

I made another try and managed a passable whisper: "Listen to me, Johnny. Listen hard, because once is all you're likely to get it. This whole thing was a fix—a trick to get you dead. Because as long as you were alive, they couldn't touch your world. The men here were never in danger. At least they weren't meant to be. But there was a change in plan. But that's only after you're taken

83

care of. And if you're alive . . ." It was getting too complicated.

"Never mind that," I said. "You outsmarted 'em. Outsmarted all of us. You're alive after all. Now the trick is to stay that way. So you lie low. There's heat and emergency food stores here, all you need until pickup. And then you'll have it made. There was a jammed solenoid, you understand? You know what a solenoid looks like? And you freed it. You saved the men. You'll be a hero. They won't dare touch you then. . . ."

"You are badly hurt, Carl Patton—"

"My name's not Carl Patton, damn you! It's Ulrik! I'm a hired killer, understand? I came here to finish you—"

"You have lost much blood, Ulrik. Are there medical supplies here?"

"Nothing that will help me. I took a power gun blast in the hip. My left thigh is nothing but bone splinters and hamburger. The suit helped me some— but not enough. But forget that. What's important is that they don't know you're alive! If they sneak back for another look and discover you—before the relief crew gets here—then they win. And they can't win, understand? I won't let 'em!"

"At my house there is a medical machine, Ulrik," Big Boy told me. "Doctors placed it there, after the Sickness. It can heal you."

"Sure—and at med center they'd have me dancing the Somali in thirty-six hours. And if I'd stayed away, I wouldn't have been in this fix at all! Forget all that and concentrate on staying alive. . . ."

I must have faded out then, because the next I knew someone was sticking dull knives in my side. I got my eyelids up and saw my suit open

and lots of blood. Big Johnny was doing things to
my leg. I told him to leave me alone, but he went
on sawing at me with red-hot saws, pouring hot
acid into the wounds. And then after a while I was
coming up from a long way down, looking at my
leg, bandaged to the hip with tape from the first
aid locker.

"You have much strength left, Ulrik," he said.
"You fought me like the frost-demon."

I wanted to tell him to let it alone, let me die in
peace, but no sound came out. The giant was on
his feet, wrapped in purple and green fur. He
squatted and picked me up, turned to the port. I
tried again to yell, to tell him that the play now
was to salvage the only thing left: revenge. That
he'd had his turn at playing Saint Bernard to the
rescue, that another hopeless walk in the snow
would only mean that Podnac and Illini had won
after all, that my bluff had been for nothing. But it
was no use. I felt him stagger as the wind hit him,
heard my suit thermostat click on. Then the cotton-
wool blanket closed over me.

29

I don't remember much about the trip back. The suit's metabolic monitors kept me doped—those and nature's defenses against the sensation of being carried over a shoulder through a blizzard, while the bone chips separated and began working their way through the crushed flesh of my thigh. Once I looked into the big frost-scarred face, met the pain-dulled eyes.

"Leave me here," I said. "I don't want help. Not from you, not from anybody. I win or lose on my own."

He shook his head.

"Why?" I said. "Why are you doing it?"

"A man," he said. "A man.. . must do . . . what he sets out to do."

He went on. He was a corpse, but he wouldn't lie down and die.

I ate and drank from the tubes in my mouth from reflex. If I'd been fully awake I'd have starved myself to shorten the ordeal. Sometimes I was conscious for a half an hour at a stretch, knowing how a quarter of beef felt on the butcher's hook; and other times I slept and dreamed I had passed the entrance exams for Hell. A few times I was

aware of falling, of lying in the snow, and then of
big hands that painfully lifted, grunting; of the big,
tortured body plodding on.

Then there was another fall, somehow more
final than the others. For a long time I lay where I
was, waiting to die. And after a while it got
through to me that the suit wouldn't let me go as
easily as that. The food and the auto-drugs that
would keep a healthy man healthy for a year would
keep a dying man in torture for almost as long. I
was stuck on this side of the river, like it or not. I
opened my eyes to tell the giant what I thought of
that, but didn't see him: what I did see was his
house, looming tall against the big trees a hundred
yards away. It didn't take me more than a day to
crawl to it. I did it a hundred miles at a time, over
a blanket of broken bottles. The door resisted for a
while, but in the end I got my weight against it
and it swung in and dumped me on the plank floor.
After that there was another long, fuzzy time while
I clawed my way to the oversized med cabinet, got
it opened, and fell inside. I heard the diagnostic
unit start up, felt the sensors moving over me.
Then I didn't know any more for a long, long
time.

30

This time I came out of it clearheaded, hungry, pain-free, and with a walking cast on my leg. I looked around for my host, but I was all alone in the big lodge. There was no cheery blaze on the hearth, but the house was as hot as a skid-row flop in summertime. At some time in the past, the do-gooders had installed a space heater with automatic controls to keep the giant cozy if the fire went out. I found some food on the shelves and tried out my jaws for the first time in many days. It was painful, but satisfying. I fired up the comm rig and got ready to tell the Universe my story. Then I remembered there were still a few details to clear up. I went to the door with a vague idea of seeing if Johnny Thunder was outside, chopping wood for exercise. All I saw was a stretch of wind-packed snow, the backdrop of giant trees, the gray sky hanging low overhead like wet canvas. Then I noticed something else: an oblong drift of snow, halfway between me and the forest wall.

The sound of snow crust crunching under my feet was almost explosively loud in the stillness as I walked across to the long mound. He lay on his back, his eyes open to the sky, glazed over with ice. His arms were bent at the elbow, the hands open as if he were carrying a baby. The snow was drifted over him, like a blanket to warm him in his sleep. The dog was beside him, frozen at her post.

I looked at the giant for a long time, and words stirred inside me: things that needed a voice to carry them across the gulf wider than space to where he had gone. But all I said was: "You made it, Johnny. We were the smart ones; but you were the one that did what you set out to do."

31

I flipped up the SEND key, ready to fire the blast that would sink Podnac and crew like a lead canoe; but then the small, wise voice of discretion started whispering at me. Nailing them would have been a swell gesture for me to perform as a corpse, frozen with a leer of triumph on my face, thumbing my nose from the grave. I might even have had a case for blowing them sky-high to save Johnny Thunder's frozen paradise for him, in view of the double-cross they'd tried on me.

But I was alive, and Johnny was dead. And six million was still waiting. There was nothing back at the pod that couldn't be explained in terms of the big bad scorpion that had gnawed my leg.

Johnny would be a hero, and they'd put up a nice marker for him on some spot the excavating rigs didn't chew up—I'd see to that.

In the end I did the smart thing, the shrewd thing. I told them what they wanted to hear; that the men were safe, and that the giant had died a hero like a giant should. Then I settled down to wait for the relief boat.

32

I collected. Since then I've been semi-retired. That's a nice way of saying that I haven't admitted to myself that I'm not taking any more assignments. I've spent my time for the past year traveling, seeing the sights, trying out the luxury spots, using up a part of the income on the pile I stashed away. I've eaten and drunk and wenched and sampled all the kicks from air-skiing to deep-sea walking, but whatever it is I'm looking for, I have a hunch I won't find it, any more than the rest of the drones and thrill-seekers will.

It's a big, impersonal Universe, and little men crave the thing that will give them stature against the loom of stars.

But in a world where once there was a giant, the rest of us are forever pygmies.

NO SHIP BOOTS
IN FAIRYLAND

CHAPTER ONE

"Mr. Vallant!" the sharp voice of full Professor Wormwell cut like a blade across the straying thoughts of pre-astro registrant 37537978, known to himself as Amory Vallant. He looked up to meet the glare of the plump little professor's smallish, pale-blue eyes.

"May I presume, Mr. Vallent," the lecturer said, icily sardonic, "to inquire at what point in my remarks you ceased listening—?"

"What makes you think I *stopped* listening, Wormy?" Vallant heard himself say. He listened helplessly as his voice persisted: "to stop listening I'd have to start listening first. And I've heard all that tired old propanganda before, lots of times. I grew up right here in the Complex, remember?" He let it go at that, knowing with a sinking feeling that he had put his neck all the way in, at last.

Wormwell's plump face had turned a dangerous red, then paled. His torn-pocket mouth in which, curiously, his teeth didn't show, was half-open. Vallant was only peripherally aware of the rest of the class staring at him with astonished expressions.

"I was saying," the words seemed to issue from Wormwell's mouth without his volition, "that without the technology so happily bestowed upon us by the Niss, our planet would today be unfit for human habitation, by reason of over-population, pollution of air and water, depletion of natural resources, and social conflict. The record of our decline during the decades immediately prior to the advent of our great benefactors clearly shows that with all these self-destructive trends accelerating, by the turn of the last century, only twenty years ago, all would have been up with the human race! A sad end, people, to five billion years of organic and cultural evolution. But that end was aborted and by the timely intervention of our friends, and it is to them alone that each of you owes his personal survival, the riches of our present over-crowded but viable society, the unlimited potentialities of the human-Niss future!'' Wormwell's eyes fixed again on #37537978. ''Consider that, Mr. Vallant, when you find yourself fretting under the minimal restraints upon your personal whims imposed by the Syndarch for the greater good of all!''

''Sure,'' Vallant agreed. ''They're great fellows, the Niss: they let us stay on and fester in the rotting remains of our cities, and even go through the motions of developing out pitiful little Space Sciences, like this silly so-called course in Solar navigation, and the Pluto probe; Pluto, for Ford's sake! We haven't even checked out Callisto! The Niss are interested in Pluto, maybe, but somehow we never quite get to do what *we* want—like clearing out of his decayed megalops and building a Lunar colony.''

There was a stir near the side door of the classroom, and a Niss came in, a grotesque five-foot figure with a deeply seamed, gray-green hide, pinkish crest fully erect, ruby-red eyes which glittered from crater-like sockets in the scaled face. The alien raised a lean arm and pointed all four knobby fingers at Vallant.

"That one," it hissed, with a flash of red tongue in the cotton mouth. "Take that one!" The Niss stood waiting, the ring of students surrounding it giving ground uneasily as its gaze flicked from one to another.

"What, are you accomplices of the wrecker?" the monitor's hiss rose to a higher pitch. "Must I designate *all* of you for Correction?" Instantly it had spoken, the alien realized its mistake: by its threat it had converted the crowd from the status of ally to that of co-victim. In haste it again directed its curiously disturbing four-fingered gesture at Vallant, like a four-pronged spear poised for the thrust.

"That man is a fool," it said harshly. "Reared and sustained by the generosity of the Syndarch, and even offered the riches of higher education and the prospect of a commission in the Terran Fleet, he turns on the fostering hand and insults the benefactor! I tell you all, he *is* a fool!"

"Maybe so," a husky redhead spoke up from behind the Niss, "but I agree with him. We could do better without any Niss around." Before the Niss could turn to confront this threat, the stocky student brought down an overhand chop to the creature's scaled neck. It collapsed, its forked tongue flicking out in a fruitless reflexive effort to assess the danger that had killed it. The lean limbs twitched and became still; a trickle of thin, greenish fluid ran from the lipless mouth.

At the sudden violence, the students recoiled, while from the podium Wormwell uttered a yell of indignation.

"Stay back, don't touch it," the redhead commanded as two girls bent over the fallen alien solicitously; his eyes went to the professor.

"Let's clear out of here and scatter," he told the students. "We'll leave this thing for Professor Wormy. He'll think up an explanation: it's his neck if he doesn't. And remember: act astonished when you hear about a Niss having an accident." He turned abruptly and left the room. Vallant stared after him for a moment, then followed with the rest.

"Jason," Vallant called after the redhead. "Wait up. I appreciate you siding with me, but maybe you went a little too far."

The redhead paused as Vallant overtook him. "That's our problem," he said, still flushed and angry with the impulse that had killed the sacrosanct alien. "We're too restrained. It's time to start doing something."

"What will you do now?" Vallant asked.

"I'm thinking about the Navy, Ame," Able replied. "I could enlist, work my way up. I don't need to wait for an ROTC commission."

"That's a tough life," Vallant commented. "But maybe you're right; it would get you out of the area fast."

"Maybe; I might even luck into a spot on the Pluto Rescue Mission."

"What's that?"

"Haven't you heard?" Transmissions from the manned Pluto probe have stopped."

"That's bad," Vallant said. "Our first and only space effort in a century—it *has* to succeed. Anyway—good luck." They shook hands and hurried off in different directions.

2

It was late. Vallant had been walking for hours, and was only a block from his apartment. The third level walkaway was deserted except for a lone Niss standing under the glare of a polyarc fifty feet ahead. Vallant hurried along, as if intent on the voice of the newser from the tiny tri-D set he carried:

". . . perturbation in the motion of Pluto. Before transmission was interrupted, the reports from the Survey Party confirmed that the ninth planet has left its orbit and has entered a spiral orbit toward the Sun. Dr. Vetenskap, expedition head, said that no explanation can be offered for the phenomenon. Calculations indicate that although Pluto will cross the orbit of the Earth in approximately forty-five years, an actual collision is unlikely; however serious consequences could follow a close passage of the body . . ."

Vallant turned the audio up. Ahead, the immobile Niss was staring at him with small, red eyes.

". . . inexplicable disappearance from Pluto of the Survey scouting vessel," the newser was saying. "The boat's crew, operating in the northern hemisphere of the uninhabited planet, had left it in order to take Solar observations; the stranded men, rescued by the main party after a three-day ordeal, stated that they observed the scout to rise, apparently under full control, and ascend to extreme altitude before being lost from view. The boat was fully fueled, and capable of an extended voyage. The Patrol is on the look-out for the stolen vessel, but so far—"

As Vallant came abreast of the waiting Niss, it moved suddenly into his path, reached out its four-fingered parody of a human hand, twitched the set from his grip and with a convulsive motion, crushed it flat.

"Here, what the devil—" Vallant started. But the Niss had already tossed the ruin aside, and turned away to resume its immobile stance under the glare of the light.

Vallant stared at the creature, the dusty gray-green hide, furrowed like an alligator's, the flacid crest that drooped over one pin-point eye, the dun-colored tunic and drab leather straps that hung loosely on the lean, five-foot body.

He took a step; the Niss turned its narrow head to face him. The tiny eyes glittered like rubies.

"Why did you smash my trideo?" Vallant said angrily.

The Niss stared for a moment longer; then it opened its mouth—a flash of snow-white in the gloom—and flicked a tongue like a scarlet worm past snake-teeth in an unmistakable gesture.

Vallant doubled a fist. Instantly, the Niss flipped

back the corner of its hip-length cape, exposing
the butt of a pistol-like apparatus with a flared
muzzle.

Vallant locked eyes with the alien; the words of
the ten-times-daily public service announcement
came back to him:

"Remember—it is our privilege to welcome the
Niss among us as honored guests, who share their
vast knowledge with us freely, to the betterment of
all mankind."

The Niss stood, waiting. Vallant, fists still
clenched, turned and walked away. The Niss let
him go—so it appeared Wormy had succeeded in
his coverup.

3

At the door to his apartment block Vallant took
out his electro-key, pressed it in the slot. From
behind him there was a tiny sound, a whistling
cough. Vallant turned; a wizened face on a turkey
neck peered at him.

"Ame," a voice as thin as smoke said. "Lord,
boy, you look wonderful . . ." The old man came
closer, stood round-shouldered, one veined hand
clutching the lapels of an oddly-cut coat. A few
strands of wispy, colorless hair crossed the age-

freckled skull. White stubble covered the sagging cheeks; the pale lines of old scars showed against the crepy skin.

"Guess you don't know me, Ame . . ."

"I can't say that I do," Vallant said. "What—"

"That's all right, Ame; no way you could, I guess . . ." The old man held out a hand that trembled like a leaf in a gentle breeze. "We served in the Navy together; we've been through a lot. But you don't know. It's been a long time . . ." the wrinkled face twisted into an unreadable expression. "Longer than you'd think."

Vallant shook his head. "You must have me confused with someone else, old timer. I've never been in the Navy."

The old man nodded as though Vallant had agreed with him. "There's a lot you need to know about. That's why I came. I had to, you see? Because if I didn't, why, who knows what might happen? Best I can remember, you're liable to be in big trouble just about now."

"I don't—" Vallant started doubtfully. Had the old fellow somehow found out about the dead Niss?

"Look, Ame," the old man cut in urgently, "could we go inside?" He glanced both ways along the walkaway. "Before one of those green devils shows his ugly face . . ."

Vallant looked at the old man. "You mean the Niss?"

The old eyes were bright. "That's who I mean; but don't you worry, boy, we'll take care of them—"

"That's careless talk, grandad. The Syndarch

frowns on unfriendly remarks about our honored guests, in case you'd forgotten.''

"Strange, Ame . . ." the old man shook his head. "But I've got no time now to waste thinking about that. There's things we've got to do . . ." He fumbled in his coat. "I need help . . ."

"If you're a former Navy man, the Society will take care of you," Vallant said.

"Not money; I've got all I need." He took out a much-folded paper, opened it with shaking hands, handed it across to Vallant. It was a map, creased and patched, grimy and oil-spattered. The legend in the corner read:

TERRESTRIAL SPACE ARM—POLAR PROJECTION. Sol IX March 2212.

He noticed the date, some years in the future, but made no comment.

"I know this is hard to take, just sprung on you like this, Ame," the old man said. "You're not ready for it yet, but later. . . ."

The old man leaned, pointing. "See this spot right here? A river cuts through the mountains—a river of liquid nitrogen. The gorge is a thousand feet deep—and the falls come thundering down out of the sky like the end of the world. That's the place, Ame. They'd kill to get it, make no mistake—and that's be only the beginning." He folded the map almost reverently and put it away.

"Who'd kill?" Vallant demanded.

"The sneaking, filthy, Niss, boy—who else?" the old man's voice snapped with an echo of youthful authority. "They trailed me in, of course. You heard about the stolen Survey boat?"

Vallant frowned, nodding. "You mean the one that disappeared on Pluto?"

The ancient head nodded quickly. "That's right, that was me. Lucky, them boys coming down like they did. Otherwise, I'd have had another thirty-odd years to wait. Might not of made it. I figured to lose them, but I'm getting old; not as sharp as I used to be. I killed one an hour ago. Don't know how long I've got—"

"You *killed* a Niss?"

"Not the first one, either." The old man's toothless grin was cheerful. "Now, what I have to tell you, Ame—"

"Look . . ." Vallant's voice was low. "I don't know what you think you've got on me, but it won't work. I won't turn you in—but you can't stay here. God knows I have no use for the Niss, but killing one—"

The old man looked into Vallant's face, searchingly. "You *are* Amory Vallant . . ?"

"That's right. I don't know how you know my name, but—" Vallant broke off, wondering how much more the old man knew.

"Look here, Ame. I know it's hard to understand. And I guess I wander; getting old . . ." He fumbled over his pockets, brought out a warped packet, paper-wrapped, passed it over to Vallant.

"Go ahead—take a look."

4

Vallant unfolded the wrappings, took out a once-glossy tri-D photo. It showed a line of men in regulation ship-suits standing against a curving wall of metal. The next was a shot of a group of boyish-faced men in identical Aerospace blue blouses, sitting at a long table, forks raised toward mouths. In another, two men stood on a stormy hillside scattered with the smoking fragment of a wrecked ship.

Vallant looked up, puzzled. "What—"

"Look closer, Ame. Look at the faces." The old man's bony finger reached, indicated a man in a worn uniform, looking down at torn metal. He had a lean face, short-cropped sandy hair, deep-set eyes—

"Hey!" Vallant said. "That looks like my dad—but he was killed in '03."

"Not your pa, Ame: you. In the other ones, too. . . ." The old man crouched forward, watching Vallant's face as he shuffled through the pictures. There he was—standing on the bridge of a capital ship, clip-board in hand; leaning on a bar, holding a glass, an arm over the shoulders of a redheaded man; posing stiffly before a bazaar stall

manned by a sullen Niss with his race's unfortunate expression of permanent guilt stamped on the
gray-green features.

Vallant stared at the old man. "I've never been
in the Navy—I never saw the inside of a ship of
the line—I was never on the Niss-world . . !" He
flipped through the remaining pictures. "Here's
one where I've got gray hair and a commodore's
star! How the devil did you fake these up, old-
timer?"

"They're no fakes, Ame. Look there—that redheaded young fellow—do you know him?"

Vallant studied the picture. "I have a friend
named Able; Jason Able—at Unitech; we're both
students there. This looks like him—only older."

The old man was nodding, grinning. "That's
right, Ame. Jase Able." The grin faded abruptly.
"But I didn't come here to talk about old times—"

"Is he a relative of yours?"

"Not exactly. Listen; my boat; they got it. Didn't
have time to camouflage it like I planned. It's at
the Granyauck Navy Yard now; I saw it yesterday.
We've got to have that boat, Ame; it's the fastest
model there is—you know how to handle her?"

"I guess so—I'm an Astronautics major. But
you're way ahead of me; hold on a minute. How
do you know me? And where did you get those
pictures? What's the map all about? Why did you
kill a Niss—and what's this about a boat? You
know the Syndarch outlawed private space travel
thirty years ago. . . !"

"Hold on, Ame . . .." The old man wiped a
trembling hand across his forehead. "I guess I'm
going too fast—but I have to hurry. There's no
time—"

"Start with the boat. Are you saying you stole it and came here from Pluto?"

"That's right, Ame. I—"

"That's impossible. Nobody could stay alive on Pluto. And anyway the Patrol or the Niss would stop any ship—"

"It's the same thing; the Syndarch is just the traitors that made peace with the Niss after the War—"

"War?"

"You don't even know about the War, do you?" The old man looked confused. He tottered, and Vallant caught his arm, held him upright. "So much to tell, Ame—and no time," the old fellow gasped. "We've got to hurry. The War—not much of a fight to it; it was maybe thirty years ago; our first manned ships were just starting their probes out beyond Big Jupe. The Niss hit us; rolled us up like a rug. What the hell, we didn't have a chance; our ships were nothing but labs, experimental models, unarmed. The Niss offered a deal. Ramo took 'em up on it. The public never even knew. Now the Niss have occupied Earth for twenty-five years—"

"Occupied! But . . . they're supposed to be our honored guests—"

"That's the Syndarch line. As for why I came back, I had to Ame. I had to tell you about Galliale and the Portal—about the history of the world—of all the worlds!"

"Slow down, old fellow; start at the beginning—"

"I could have stayed . . ." the old man's eyes were distant, the present forgotten. "But I couldn't chance it . . ." he seemed to pull himself together with an effort. "And anyway, I kind of missed the old life; there's no place for ship-boots in fairyland."

5

Once inside Vallant's tiny, but neat Class IV (student) apartment, he eased the old fellow into the softest chair, brought him a cup of hot vegepap which the wizened oldster seized eagerly, and swallowed hastily.

"Don't taste like nothing—'cept maybe library paste, thinned some," he commented, "but it sure was good. But I can't go eating up your ration, Ame. Need to sleep, anyways."

Before Vallant could reply, there was a buzz from the front entry. The old man struggled to his feet, stared around the room, his lips working. "They're here already. I thought I'd thrown 'em off; I thought I was clear. . . ."

"Hold on, old timer, it's probably just a friend; sit down—"

"Any back way out of here, Ame?" The old man's eyes were desperate. From the door, the buzz sounded insistently.

"You think it's the police?"

"It's them or the Niss. I know, boy."

Vallant hesitated a moment, then went quickly to the bedroom, into the closet, felt over the wall. A panel dropped, fell outward; a framed opening showed dark beyond it.

"I discovered this when they were doing some work on the other side," he told his guest. "It's one advantage of cracker-box construction. I phoned in a complaint, but they never fixed it. It opens into a utility room in the Municipal Admin block."

The old man hurried forward. "I'm sorry I got you into this, Ame. I won't come here again—you come to my place—the Stellar Castle on 900th— room 1196b. I've been away two days now. I've got to get back—don't tell 'em anything—and be sure you're not followed. I'll be waiting." He ducked through the opening.

From the next room there was the sound of heavy pounding—then of splintering plastic. Vallant hastily clipped the panel back in place, turned as a thick, dark man with an egg-bald head slammed through the doorway. He wore tight-cuffed, black trousers and there was a bright-metal servitude bracelet with a Syndarch escutcheon on his left wrist. His small, coal-black eyes darted around the room.

"Where's the old man?" he rapped out in a voice like bullets hitting a plank.

"Who are you? What's the idea of smashing my door?"

"You know the penalty for aiding a traitor to the Syndarch?" The intruder went past Vallant, stared around the room.

"There's nobody here," Vallant said. "And

even the Syndarch has no right to search without a warrant.''

The bald man eyes Vallant. "You telling me what rights the Syndarch's got?'' He barked a short laugh, cut it off suddenly to glare coldly at Vallant.

"Watch your step. We'll be watching you now.'' Beyond the door, Vallant caught a glimpse of a dull Niss face.

"That reminds me,'' he said. "The Niss owe me a tri-D set; one of them smashed mine today.''

The beady eyes bored into him, weighing whether or not to strike him. Vallant looked steadily back. "Yeah,'' the Syndarch man said. "We'll be watching you.'' He stepped past the smashed door.

As soon as he was gone, Vallant went to the closet and removed the panel.

CHAPTER TWO

Vallant stepped through the opening, fitted the panel back in place, felt his way past brooms and cans of cleaning compound, eased the door open, emerged into a dim-lit corridor. Lights showed behind a few doors along its shadowy length. He went toward a red exit light; a lone maintenance man shot him a sour look but said nothing. He pushed out through a rotating door onto the littered walkaway to the shabby section near the Gendye Tower. Here, near the center of the city, there were a few pedestrians out; a steady humming filled the air from the wheelways above. Between them, Vallant caught a glimpse of a bleary moon gleaming unnoticed in the remote sky.

It took Vallant half an hour to find the dark sideway where a dowdy plastic front adorned with a tarnished sunburst huddled between later, taller structures whose lower levels were darkened by the blight that washed about the bases of the city's towers like an overflowing sewer. Vallant stepped through a wide glass door that opened creakily before him, crossed to the dust-grimed directory, keyed the index; out-of-focus print flickered on the screen. Jason Able was registered in room 1196b. OK so far.

Vallant stepped into the ancient mechanical lift;
its door closed tiredly. Everything about the Stellar
Castle seemed ready to sigh and give up.

On the hundred-and-tenth floor he stepped out,
followed arrows to a warped plastic door against
which dull fluorescent numerals gleamed faintly.
He tapped; the door swung inward. He stepped
inside.

It was a mean, narrow room with one crowded,
dirt-glazed window, opening onto an air-shaft
through which the bleak light of a polyarc filtered.
There was a bunk bed, unmade, a wall locker with
its door ajar, its shelves empty, and beyond, a
tiny toilet cubicle. A hinge-sprung suitcase lay
near the bed. The old man lay on his back on the
floor. The waxy face, thin-nosed, sunken-cheeked,
stared up at him with eyes as remote as a statue of
Pharaoh.

Vallant touched the bony wrist; it was as cool
and inert as modeling clay. The packet of pictures
lay scattered on the floor. Vallant felt inside the
coat; the map was gone. He went to the locker;
there was a covered birdcage on its floor among
curls of dust, a small leather case beside it. He
went back to the bed and checked the suitcase; it
contained worn garments of strange cut, a leather
folder with six miniature medals, a few more edge-
crimped photos, a toy cross-bow, beautifully made,
and a Browning 2mm needler.

A tiny sound brought Vallant upright; he reached
for the needler, searching the gloom. From somewhere above him, a soft scraping sounded. Among
the shadows under the ceiling, two tiny amber
lights glinted; something small and dark moved.
Vallant flipped the pistol's safety off—

A shape no bigger than a cat dropped to the bed with an almost noiseless thump.

"You are Jason's friend," a piping voice said. "Did you come to help me?"

CHAPTER THREE

It was almost man-shaped, with large eyes which threw back crimson highlights, oversized fox-like ears, a sharp nose; it wore form-fitting clothing of a dark olive color which accentuated its thin limbs and knobby joints. Dark hair grew to a widow's peak on its forehead. It stood on two legs, waiting for an answer.

"What are you?" Vallant's voice was a hoarse whisper.

"I'm Jimper." The tiny voice was like the peeping of a chick. "The Not-men came. Jason is dead; now who will help Jimper?" The little creature moved toward Vallant. There was a jaunty cap on the doll-sized head; a broken feather trailed from it.

"Who killed the old man?"

"Are you his friend?"

"He seemed to think so."

"There was a large man—great in the belly, and with splendid clothing, though he smelled of burning drug-weed. Two of the Not-men were with him. They struck Jason a mighty blow, and afterward they took things from his clothes. I was afraid; I hid among the rafters."

"What are you—a pet?"

The little creature stood straighter.

"I am the Ambassador of the King. I came with Jason to see the king of the Giants."

Vallant pocketed the gun. "I've been to a lot of places; I never saw anything like you before. Where did you come from?"

"My Land of Galliale lies beyond the place of Blue Ice—the world you know as Pluto."

"Pluto? Out there the atmosphere falls as snow every winter. Nothing could live there."

"Green and fair lies Galliale beyond the ice." The little figure crept closer to the foot of the bed. "Jason is dead. Now Jimper is alone. Let me stay with you, Jason's friend."

"Sorry, I don't need a pet."

"I am the Ambassador of the King!" the manni-kin piped. "Do not leave me alone," he added, his tiny voice no more than a cricket's chirp.

"Do you know why they killed the old man?"

"He knew of the Portal—and my Land of Galliale. Long have the Not-men sought it—"

The tiny head came up suddenly; the long nose twitched. "The Not-men," the bird voice shrilled. "They come . . .!"

Vallant stepped to the door, listened. "I don't hear anything."

"They come—from below. Three of them, and evil are their thoughts."

"You're a mind-reader, too?"

"I feel the shapes of their intentions . . ." the tiny voice was frantic. "Flee, Jason's friend; they wish you harm . . ."

"What about you?"

"Jason made a carrying box for me—there—in the locker."

Vallant grabbed up the birdcage, put it on the bed; the Ambassador of the King crept inside.

"My cross-bow," he called; "it lies in Jason's box; and my knapsack."

Vallant retrieved the miniature weapon and the pack, handed them in to their owner.

"All right, Jimper. I'm not sure I'm not dreaming you—but I'd hate to wake up and find out I wasn't."

"Close are they now," the small voice shrilled. "They come from there . . ." He pointed along the gloomy hallway. Vallant went in the opposite direction. He glanced back from the first cross-corridor; three Niss stepped from the elevator; he watched as they went to the room he had just left, pushed inside.

"It looks as though you know what you're talking about, Jimper," Vallant said. "Let's get away from here before the excitement begins."

CHAPTER FOUR

There was a scattering of late-shift workers hurrying through the corridor when Vallant reached the secret entry to his flat. He waited until they had hustled out of sight, then opened the utility room door, stepped inside. In the cage, Jimper moaned softly.

"The Feared Men," he peeped.

Vallant stood stock-still. He put his ear against the removable panel. A heavy voice sounded from beyond it:

"How did I know he'd die so easy? I had to make him talk, didn't I?"

"Fool!" hissed a voice like gas escaping under pressure. "Little will he talk now."

"Look, your boss isn't going to blame me, is he?"

"You will die, and I with you."

"Huh? You mean—just because—"

There was a sudden hiss, then a sound of rattling paper. "Perhaps this will save our lives," the Niss voice said. "The map . . .!"

In the cage, Jimper whined. "I fear the Notmen," he piped. "I fear the smell of hate."

Vallant raised the cage to eye-level. The little creature inside blinked large, anxious eyes at him.

"They found the old man's map," Vallant said. "He had it in his pocket. Was it important?"

"The map?" Jimper stood, gripping the bars of the cage. "Vallant—with the map they can seek out my Land of Galliale, and fall upon us, unsuspecting! They must not have it!"

"They've already got it—and if I'd walked in the front door, they'd have had me too. I'm in trouble, Jimper. I've got to get away, hide out somewhere . . .

"First, the map, Vallant!"

"What do you mean?"

"We must take it from them. You are a Giant, like them; can you not burst in and take it from them?"

"I'm afraid heroics are out of my line, Jimper. Sorry, but—"

"Jason died for the map, Vallant. He came to warn you, and they killed him. Will you let them take it now?"

Vallant rubbed his jaw. "I've gotten mixed up in something I don't understand. I don't know the old man; he never got around to saying why he came to see me—"

"To save a world, Vallant—perhaps a Galaxy. And now only you can help!"

"The map is that important, is it?"

"More than you could know! You must make a plan, Vallant!"

Vallant nodded. "I guess my number's up anyway; I'd never get clear of the city, with the Syndarch and the Niss after me. I might as well go down fighting." He chewed his lip. "Listen, Jimper. I want you to sneak around front, with my key. You can reach the key-hole if you climb up on the railing. When you plug it in, the buzzer will go. Then I'll move in and hit them on the flank. Maybe I can put it over. Can you do it?''

Jimper looked out through the brass bars of the birdcage. "It is a fearsome thing to walk abroad among the Giants . . ." He gripped his five-inch cross-bow. "But if you ask it, Vallant, I will try.''

"Good boy." Vallant put the cage on the floor, opened it. Jimper stepped out, stood looking up at the man. Briefly, Vallant described the location of his apartment entry; he handed over the electro-key, which Jimper slung over his shoulder by its thong.

"Be careful," Vallant cautioned earnestly. "There may be somebody watching the place from outside. If you make it, give it one good shove and leave it and run like hell; I'll meet you back here. If I don't show up in ten minutes, you're on your own.''

Jimper stood straight; he settled his cap on his head.

"I am the Ambassador of the King," he said. "I shall do my best, Vallant.''

2

Vallant waited, his ear to the thin panel. The two who lay in wait inside conversed excitedly, in low tones.

"Look," the man said. "The guy's wise we're after him. He won't come back here; we've got to get the map to the Syndarch—"

"To the Uttermagnate!"

"The Syndarch's *my* boss—"

"He is as dirt beneath the talons of the Uttermagnate!"

Faintly, the door buzzer sounded. The voices ceased abruptly. Then:

"OK, you cover him as he comes in; I clip him back of the ear . . ."

Vallant waited a quarter of a minute; then he pushed on the panel, caught it as it leaned into the room, stepped in after it, silently, the gun in his hand. He crossed quickly to the connecting doorway to the outer room. The man and the Niss stood across the room on either side of the entry, heads cocked alertly; the alien held a gun, the man a heavy sap.

"Don't move!" Vallant snapped, hardening his voice.

The two whirled on him like clockwork soldiers.
Vallant jumped aside, fired as the Niss burned the
door-frame by his ear. The Browning snarled; the
alien slammed back, fell, a cluster of needles bright
against the leathery hide. The man dropped the
length of weighted hose, raised his hands.

"Don't shoot . . . !" he choked. Vallant went
to him, lifted the map from his pocket.

"Talk fast!" Vallant snapped. "Who's the old
man?"

"All I know is," the man stuttered, "the Niss
boss said bring the old guy in."

"You tailed him here, but he lost you. How'd
you get to him?"

"There was four teams working him. Mullo
picked him up on One Level."

"Why'd you kill him?"

"It was an accident—"

"Why'd you come back for me?"

"Once the old guy was dead, you was the only
lead . . ."

"Lead to what?"

Sweat popped out on the man's veined temples.
He had a narrow, horsey face, a long torso with
too-short legs.

"I . . . dunno. They said look for a map; it was
something they wanted."

"You take orders from . . . those?" Vallant
glanced at the dead Niss.

"I do like I'm told," the man said sullenly.

"You know any prayers?"

The man's face broke like smoke in a gust of
wind. He fell to his knees, clasped his hands in a
grotesque parody of adoration. He babbled. Vallant
stood over him, eyeing the thick, acne-scarred
neck, the short-clipped hair, with dandruff.

"I ought to kill you—for my own protection," he said. "But that's where you skunks have the advantage . . ." He hit the man hard behind the ear with the gun-butt; he fell on his face. Vallant trussed him with a maroon bathrobe cord, knotted a handkerchief over his mouth, then rose, looked around at the laden bookshelves, the music storage unit, the ration-stocked pantry beyond.

"It was nice while it lasted," he muttered. He went to the closet, stepped through into the dark room beyond.

"Jimper!" he called. There was no answer. The cage was empty, the tiny knapsack beside it. He picked it up, stepped out into the corridor, went to the exit, out into the walkaway, turned back toward the entrance to the apartment block.

3

As he passed the dark mouth of a narrow serviceway, a sudden *thump!* sounded, followed by a squeal like a rusty hinge. Vallant whirled; a giant rat lay kicking long-toed hind feet, a three inch length of wooden dowel projecting from its chest. Beyond it lay a second rat, its yellow chisel-teeth closed on a shaft which had entered its mouth and emerged under its left shoulder. Vallant took a step into the alley; a foot-long rodent darted at him. He pivoted, swung a foot, sent it thudding against the wall, whirled in time to see Jimper, his back to the wall, loose a bolt from his bow, then toss the weapon aside and draw a two-inch dagger. A red-eyed rodent rushed him; he danced aside, struck—

Vallant snatched him up, aimed a kick at the rodent, quickly retreated to the dim-lit walkaway.

"I'm sorry, Jimper; I forgot about the rats . . ."

"My . . . bow . . ." Jimper keened. His head drooped sideways. Vallant was suddenly aware of the lightness of the small body; there seemed to be only bones under the silken-soft garments.

"How long since you've had a meal?"

"Jason gave Jimper food . . . before he went away . . ."

"You mean you waited there two days, in the dark, without food and water?"

Jimper stirred, tried to raise his head. "Jimper is tired . . ."

The elfin face was grayish, the eyes hollow.

"You've had a tough time, partner," Vallant said. "But I can't guarantee it won't get tougher."

Vallant walked back up the alley, recovered the cross-bow. The rats were gone—even the two dead ones, dragged away by their fellows.

"I'll get you some food," Vallant said; "then maybe you can tell me what this is all about."

"Then . . . you will help Jimper?"

"I don't know, Jimper. I just killed a Niss, and gave a Syndarch man a severe headache. I'm afraid I've permanently spoiled my popularity in this area. I have a couple of hours, maybe, before they find them. That means I'll have to make some very hurried travel arrangements. Afterwards we can discuss future plans—if we still have any. Future, I mean."

CHAPTER FIVE

Vallant stood in the angle of the security wall surrounding the Navy Yard, sheltered from the glare of the polyarcs, looking over the row of battered space-boats parked in a ragged line. "Do you know which one it is?" he whispered.

"Well I know her, Vallant; a fleet vessel; none can match her."

"Point her out to me." He lifted the cage to a shed roof, scrambled up beside it. Over the wall-top, the lights threw back dull highlights from the tarnished hulls of three Syndarch hundred-tonners squatting in an irregular row. Beyond, half a dozen of the Syndarch's private racing stable were parked, corrosion-streaked under their gaily-painted racing stripes.

Far to the right, Jimper pointed to a smaller vessel, agleam with chromalloy and vivid enamel, glistening under the polyarcs. Men worked around it; nearby stood four armed men in the pale green of the Syndarch contract police.

"I'll have to take some chances now," Vallant said softly. "You'd better stay here; I won't be able to look out for you."

"I will look out for myself, Vallant!"

"All right, partner; but this will be risky."

"What will you do, Vallant?" Jimper's voice was a mouse's squeak, but he stood with a bold stance, looking up at Vallant.

"I'm going to waltz into Operations as though I owned a controlling interest, and see what happens. Keep your fingers crossed."

"Jimper will be near, Vallant. Good luck."

Vallant stooped, put out a hand. "Thanks, partner—and if I don't make it, good luck to you—and your land of Galliale." Jimper laid his tiny hand solemnly against Vallant's palm.

"Stout heart," he piped, "and fair hunting."

2

Vallant strode through the gate, walking briskly, like a man intent on serious business. A Niss eyed him from a sentry box by the gate as he rounded the end of a building, went up steps, pushed through wide doors. He went along a carpeted corridor and under an archway into a bright room with chart-lined walls. A fat man with a high, pink forehead looked up from behind a counter, glanced at Vallant, let his bored gaze wander past. Vallant rapped smartly on the counter.

"A little service here, please, my man. I need a Clearance Order; I'm taking a boat out."

The fat man's eyes flicked back to Vallant. He
plucked a plastic toothpick from a breast pocket,
plied it on large, square teeth. "So who're you?"
he inquired in an unoiled tenor.

"I'm the Syndarch's new pilot," Vallant said
coldly. He wiped a finger across the dusty counter,
examined its tip distastefully. "I trust that meets
with your approval?"

There was an extended silence, broken only by
the click of the fat man's toothpick.

"Nobody never tells me nothing," he stated
abruptly. He turned, plucked a paper from a desk
behind him, scribbled on it, tossed it at Vallant,
and grunted.

"Where's old man Ramo going this time?"

Vallant looked at him sharply. "Mind your tone,
my man."

The toothpick fell with a tiny clatter. The fat
man's face was suddenly strained. "Hey, I din't
mean nothin'. I'm loyal, you bet." He indicated
himself with an ink-stained thumb. "Twenty-one
years a Syndarch man," he boasted.

"What was the lift-off time again?" Vallant
said briskly.

"Plenty time yet, sir." The squeaky voice was
half an octave higher. "I wasn't expecting the
pilot in fer half a hour yet. I got my paper-work all
set early, just in case, like. All you got to do, you
got to sign the flight plan." The man pointed with
the blue thumb. Vallant scribbled *Mort Furd* in the
indicated space, folded his copy and tucked it
away.

"About that crack," the fat man started.

"I'm giving you the benefit of the doubt,"
Vallant said.

3

Outside, Vallant walked quickly across to the low shed under the glare sign reading EQUIP-MENT—STATION PERSONNEL ONLY. Inside, a small man with lined, brown skin and artificial-looking hair looked at him over a well-thumbed pictonews.

"I want to draw my gear," Vallant said briskly. "I'm taking the new boat out in a few minutes."

The little man got to his feet, held out a hand expectantly.

"Let's see that Issue Order."

"I'm running late," Vallant said. "I haven't got one."

The little man sat down and snatched up his paper. "Come back when you got one," he snapped.

"You wouldn't want to be the cause of delaying Leader Ramo's departure, would you?" Vallant looked at him pointedly.

"I do my job; no tickee no washee." The little man turned a page, appeared absorbed in his reading.

"Hey," Vallant said. The man glanced up, jaw lowered for a snappy retort. He saw the gun in

Vallant's hand, froze, mouth open. "Sit tight and read your funny-book," Vallant ordered. "And maybe you won't get hurt." The magazine fell to the floor as the man complied. Vallant went around him, into the stacks.

Five minutes later, wearing a vac suit, Vallant stepped from the issue-hut—and was face to face with a heavily-built Niss holding a gun like the one Vallant had first seen at the hip of the alien who had smashed his tri-D set.

"Would you mind pointing that thing in some other direction?" Vallant said, and started to edge past the alien. It hissed, jabbed the strange gun at him.

Vallant took a deep breath, wondering how fast Niss reflexes were.

"Perhaps I'd better explain—" he started—

There was a sharp clatter behind the alien; the narrow head jerked around; Vallant took a step, hit the creature on the side of the head; it bounced backwards, went down hard on its back; the gun skidded away. Valant saw a six-inch quarrel buried almost to its full length in the leathery back. He caught the Niss by the harness, dragged it into the shadow of the shed. Jimper stepped into view.

"Well smote, Vallant!" he chirped.

"Your timing was perfect, partner!" Vallant looked toward the lighted ship. The ground crew was still at work, the guards lounging nearby.

"Here we go; make a wide swing. Wait until they're all admiring me, and then run for it." Vallant started across the open ramp with a long stride. A man with a clip-board strolled forward to meet him. Vallant flapped the Clearance Order at him.

"All set to lift?" he barked.

"Eh? Why, no; I haven't even run idling checks—" the man backed, keeping pace.

"Skip 'em; I'm in a hurry." Vallant brushed past, reached the access ladder, thumbed the lock control; it cycled open. A tiny figure bounded from shadow, leaped up, disappeared inside.

"Hey—"

"Clear the area; I'm lifting!" Vallant called over his shoulder and went up, swung through the open port, clanged it shut behind him, climbed up into the dim-lit control compartment, slid into the deep-padded acceleration couch, threw the shock frame in place. He remembered his freshman preflight course. It appeared the standard controls hadn't been updated since then.

"Get on the bunk, Jimper," he called. "Lie flat and hang on." He slammed switches. Pumps sprang into action; a whining built, merged with the rumble of preheat burners. The communicator light blinked garish red on the panel.

"You in the yacht," a harsh voice blared. "Furd, or whatever your name is—"

A Niagara of sound cut off the voice. The pressure of full emergency power crushed Vallant back in the seat. On the screen, the pattern of lights that was the port dwindled, became a smudge, then glided from view as the ship angled east, driving for Deep Space. There was no pursuit—not that Vallant could see.

"We're clear, Jimper," Vallant called. "Now all we have to do is figure out where we're going . . ."

CHAPTER SIX

Mars was a huge, glaring disk of mottled pink, crumbling at the edge into blackness, frosted white at the pole. It lit Jimper's face eerily as he perched on the edge of the chart table, watching the planet swing ponderously past on the screen.

"Not this world, Vallant!" Jimper piped again. "Jason came with me from the world of the Blue Ice—"

"You said your country was warm and green, Jimper, with a big orange sun. Let's be realistic: Pluto is only a few degrees above absolute zero. Wherever this Galliale is, it couldn't be out there."

"You must believe Jimper, Vallant." The little creature looked appealingly across at the man. "We must go to Pluto!"

"Jimper, we need supplies, information. We'll land at Aresport, rest up for a few hours and take in some of the scenery I've heard about, then see what we can find out about the old man's itinerary—"

"The Not-men will capture us!"

"Jimper, we couldn't be that important. Mars is an autonomous planet. I know commerce has been shut off for years, but the Syndarch couldn't have any influence out here—''

"Vallant—the Not-men own all the worlds! There are no Giants but those who serve them—but for those on Earth—and why they let them live, I cannot say—"

"You've got a lot of wild ideas, Jimper—"

"Look!" Jimper's finger pointed at the screen. A tiny object was visible, drifting across the center of the planetary disc. Vallant adjusted a control, locked a tracking beam on the vessel.

"If he holds that course, we're going to scrape paint . . .!" He keyed the communicator. "*Arianne* to Mars Tower West; I'm in my final approach pattern; request you clear the Sunday drivers out of the way."

"Pintail Red to Pintail One," a faint voice came from the speaker. "I think I've picked up our bogie; homing in on 23–268–6, sixteen kilo-knots . . ."

"Pintail Red, get off the clear channel, you damned fool—" the angry voice dissolved into a blur of scrambled transmission.

"Panam Patrol—out here?" Vallant twiddled controls, frowning at the instruments. "What was that course? 23—268–6 . . ." He flipped a switch; numerals glowed on the ground glass.

"Hey, Jimper—that's *us* they're talking about . . .!"

A speck separated itself from the vessel on the screen, raced toward *Arianne*.

"Hang on to your hat, Jimper," Vallant called. "He means business . . ." He slammed the drive control lever full over; the ship leaped forward.

"I guess the Ares Pavilion's out, Jimper," he said between clenched teeth, "but maybe we can find a cosy, little family-type hotel on Ganymede."

CHAPTER SEVEN

Vallant sagged over the control panel, his unshaven face hollow from the last week on short rations.

"*Arianne* to Ganymede Control," he croaked for the hundredth time. "Ganymede Control, come in . . ."

"None will answer, Vallant," Jimper piped.

"Looks like nobody home, Buddy," Vallant slumped back in the couch. "I don't understand it . . ."

"Will we go to Pluto now, Vallant?" Jimper asked anxiously, watching the unresponsive screens.

"The Not-men lie when they lead you of Earth to believe you have manned stations off-planet!" Jimper said urgently. "There is none to help us here, Vallant. We must save ourselves!"

"Driving for Deep Space is a poor way to do that," Vallant replied. "Be reasonable, Jimper. I sympathize, old fellow, but we've known for a century that Pluto is an ice-ball—its moon Chronos, too. There's no reason to expect anything else—and that's not something the Niss told us."

"Can you not trust me, Vallant?" the mannikin returned. "After all, I must have come from somewhere—and Jason told you, too."

"The old man was on his last legs," Vallant replied. "As for you, right, you have come from somewhere—but that doesn't mean the somewhere has to be Pluto."

"Why would I lie?" Jimper asked with dignity. "I am the Ambassador of the King."

"I don't say you're lying. I'm sure you believe it. But you're wrong, because it's impossible. We should turn back now, while we still have fuel enough for a landing."

"Vallant," Jimper pleaded, "turn not back, but push on, for the sake of man and Sprill alike! Never again will such an opportunity come; let us not waste it by lack of resolution. Onward! Out there, in the darkness and deep, lies the fair land of Galliale, I swear it!"

"You don't give up easily, do you, partner?" Vallant said resignedly.

Jimper sprang across, stood before Vallant, his feet planted on dial faces. "Vallant, my Land of Galliale lies beyond the snows, deep among the Blue Ice mountains. You must believe Jimper!"

"We're low on rations and my fuel banks were never intended for this kind of high-G running, weeks on end. We'll have to turn back."

"Turn back to what, Vallant? The Not-men will surely slay you—and what will happen to Jimper?"

"There's nothing out there, Jimper!" Vallant waved a hand at the screen that reflected the blackness of space, and the cold glitter of the distant stars. "Nothing but some big balls of ice called Uranus and Neptune, and the Sun's just a bright star."

"There is Pluto."

"So there is . . ." Vallant raised his head, looked

into the small, anxious face. "Where could this nice warm place of yours be, Jimper? Underground?"

"The sky of Galliale is wide and blue, Vallant, and graced with a golden sun."

"If I headed out that way—and we fail to find Galliale—that would be the end. You know that, don't you?"

"I know, Vallant. I will not lead you a-wrong."

"The old man said something about the mountains of ice; maybe—" Vallant straightened. "Well, there's nothing to go back to. I've always had a yen to see what's out there. Let's go take a look, Jimper. Maybe there are still a few undreamed of things in Heaven and Earth—or beyond them."

CHAPTER EIGHT

Days and nights passed tediously; tension changed to boredom. Vallant longed for one more chance to breath fresh air, and stretch his legs under an open sky. He changed course on the twenty-ninth day to cut across the Plutonian orbit to intercept the tiny, double world. Hours later, the planet and its big moon hung like dull-steel balls against the black; a brilliant highlight on each body threw back the glinting reflection of the tiny disc that was the distant sun.

"All right, Jimper, guide me in," Vallant said hoarsely. "It all looks the same to me."

"When we are close, then will I know." Jimper's pointed nose seemed to quiver with eagerness as he stared into the high resolution screen where Pluto loomed larger now, its surface an unrelieved white. "Soon you will see, Vallant," Jimper went on, "fair is my Land of Galliale."

"I must be crazy to use my last few ounces of reaction mass to land on that," Vallant croaked. "But it's too late now to change my mind."

For the next hours, Vallant nursed the ship along, dropping closer to the icy world. Now plains of shattered ice-slabs stretched endlessly below, rising at intervals into jagged peaks, gleaming metallically in light as eerie as that of an eclipse.

"There!" Jimper piped, pointing. "The Mountains of Blue Ice . . .!" Vallant saw the high peaks then, rising in a saw-toothed silhouette against the unending snow, their base a deep blue.

The proximity alarm clattered. Vallant pushed himself upright, read dials, adjusted the rear screen magnification. The squarish lines of a strange vessel appeared, dancing in the center of the field. Beyond, a second ship was a tiny point of reflected light.

"We're out of luck, partner," Vallant said flatly. "They must want us pretty badly. Those are fast Niss scoutboats."

"Make for the mountains, Vallant!" Jimper shrilled. "We can yet escape the Not-men!"

Vallant pulled himself together, hunched over the controls. "Ok, Jimper, I won't give up if you won't; but that's an almighty big rabbit you're going to have to pull out of that miniature hat!"

CHAPTER NINE

It was not a good landing. Vallant unstrapped himself, got to his feet, holding onto the couch for support. Jimper crept out from under the folded blankets that had fallen on him, straightening his cap.

"We're a couple of miles short of the mark, Jimper," Vallant said. "I'm sorry; it was the best I could do."

"Now must we hasten, Vallant; deep among the blue peaks lies Galliale; long must we climb." Jimper opened his knapsack, took out a tiny miniature of a standard vacuum suit, began pulling it on. Vallant managed a laugh.

"You came prepared, fella. I guess your friend Jason made that for you."

"Even in this suit, Jimper will be cold." The long nose seemed redder than ever. He fitted the grape-fruit-sized bowl in place over his head. Vallant checked the panel. The screens were dead; the proximity indicator was smashed. He checked his suit hurriedly: all OK.

"They saw us crash; they'll pick a flatter spot a few miles back; that gives us a small head start." He cycled the port open; loose objects fluttered as the air whooshed from the ship; frost formed instantly on horizontal surfaces.

Standing in the open lock, Vallant looked out at a wilderness of tilted ice-slabs, fantastic architectural shapes of frost, airy bridges, tunnels, chasms of blue ice.

"Jimper—are you sure—out there . . ?"

"High among the ice peaks," Jimper's tiny voice squeaked in Vallant's helmet. "Jimper will lead you."

"Lead on, then," Vallant jumped down into the feathery drift-snow. "I'll try to follow."

The slopes were near-vertical now, polished surfaces that slanted upward, glinting darkly. Vallant's spiked boot bit into the crumbly, dry ice. The tiny arc-white sun glared between two heights that loomed overhead like cliffs. Into the narrow valley between them, Vallant, advanced, toiled upward, Jimper scampering ahead, running easily on the ice-crust.

Far above, a mighty river poured over a high cliff, thundering down into mist: its roar was a steady rumble underfoot.

Abruptly, Jimper's voice sounded in a shrill shout. "Vallant! Success! The Gateway lies just ahead!"

Vallant struggled on another step, another, too exhausted to answer. There was a sudden muffled report, then a heavy tremor underfoot. Jimper sprang aside. Vallant looked up; far above, a vast fragment detached itself from the icewall, seeming to float downward with dream-like grace, surrounded by a convoy of lesser rubble. Triggered by a shot from below, great chunks of ice smashed against the cliff-sides, disintegrated, cascaded downward;

the main mass of the avalanch shattered, dissolved
into a cloud of ice-crystals. At the last moment,
Jimper's warning shrilling in his ears, Vallant
jumped for the shelter of a crevice. A torrent of
snow poured down through the sluice-like narrow,
quickly rising above the level of Vallant's hiding
place. His helmet rang like a bell bombarded with
gravel, then damped out as the snow packed around
him. Profound silence closed in. At least he was
well hidden. . . .

"Vallant!" Jimper's voice came through the suit's
talker. "Are you safe?"

"I don't know . . ." Vallant struggled, moved
his arms an inch. "I'm buried; no telling how
deep." He scraped at the packed snow, managed
to twist himself over on his face, then upright. He
worked carefully then, breaking pieces away from
above, thrusting them behind. He was growing
rapidly weaker; his arms seemed leaden. He rested,
dug, rested . . .

2

The harsh, white star that was the sun still hung
between the ice-cliffs when Vallant's groping fingers broke through and he pulled himself out to lie
gasping on the surface.

"Vallant—move not or you are surely lost!" Jimper piped in his ears. "Yet we are so near now. Almost were we safe, Vallant!"

He lay sprawled, too tired even to lift his head.

"The Not-men," Jimper went on. "Oh, they are close, Vallant."

"How close?" Vallant groaned.

"Close . . . close."

"Have they seen me?"

"Not yet, I think—but if you stir—"

"I can't stay here . . ." With an effort, Vallant got to his hands and knees, then rose, tottered on, slipping and falling. Above, Jimper danced on a ledge, frantic with apprehension.

"It lies just ahead!" he shrilled. "The Gateway to my Land of Galliale; only a little more, Vallant! A few scant paces . . ."

Ice chips flew from before Vallant's face. For a moment he stared, not understanding—

"They have seen you, Vallant!" Jimper screamed. "They shoot; oh, for a quiver of bolts . . .!"

Vallant turned. A hundred yards below, a party of four suited figures—men or Niss—tramped upward. One raised the gun as a warning.

"Vallant—it is not far!" Jimper shrilled. "Hasten!"

"It's no use," Vallant gasped. "You go ahead, Jimper. And I hope you find your home again, up there in the ice."

"Jimper will not desert you, Vallant! Come, rise and try again!"

Vallant made a choking sound that was half sob, half groan. He got to his feet, lurched forward; ice smashed a foot away. The concussion of the next near miss knocked him floundering into a drift of soft snow. He found his feet, struggled upward. They were shooting to intimidate, not to kill, he told himself; they needed information—and there was no escape. He crept on—and on. The four pursuers came no closer, but neither did they fall back. "They can't afford to kill us," Vallant told himself.

There was a ridge ahead; Jimper perched there; Vallant paused, gathering strength. He lunged, gained the top as another warning shot kicked a great furrow in the ice beside him; then he was sliding down the reverse slope. A dark opening showed ahead—a patch of rock, ice-free, the mouth of a cave. He rose, ran toward it, fell, then crawled . . .

It was suddenly dark; Vallant's helmet had frosted over. He groped his way on, hearing the sharp *ping!* of expanding metal.

3

"This way!" Jimper's voice rang in his helmet. "We will yet win free, Vallant!"

"Can't go . . . farther . . ." Vallant gasped. He was down again, lying on his face. He sensed a minute, but irritating tugging at his arm. Through the frost melting from his face-plate, he saw Jimper's tiny figure, pulling frantically at his sleeve. He got to his knees somehow, stood, tottered on. A powerful wind seemed to buffet at him. Wind—in this airless place . . .

Without warning, a gigantic bubble soundlessly burst; that was the sensation that Vallant felt. For a moment he stood, his senses reeling; then he shook his head, looked around, saw packed-earth walls, shored by spindly logs. Far ahead, light gleamed faintly—

A terrific blow knocked him flat. He rolled, found himself on his back, staring toward four dark figures, silhouetted against the luminous entrance through which he had come minutes before.

"I will bring rescuers!" Jimper's voice shrilled in Vallant's helmet.

"Run!" Vallant choked. "Don't let . . . them get you too . . ."

Faintness overtook him. . . .

"Do not despair, Vallant," Jimper's voice seemed faint, far away. "Jimper will return . . ."

They stood over him, three Niss, grotesque and narrow-faced in their helmets, and one human, a whiskery, small-eyed man. Their mouths worked in a conversation inaudible to Vallant. Then one of the Niss made a downward motion with its hand; the man stepped forward, reached—

Suddenly, a wooden peg stood against the gray-green fabric of the man's ship-suit, upright in the center of his chest. A second magically appeared beside it—and a third. The man toppled, clutching. . . . Behind him a Niss crouched, a flick of scarlet tongue visible against the gape of the white mouth—

A shaft stood abruptly in its throat. It fell

backward. Vallant raised his head; a troop of tiny red-and-green-clad figures stood, setting bolts and loosing them. A Niss leaped, struck down two— then stumbled, fell, his thin chest bristling with miniature quarrels. The last Niss turned, ran from sight.

"Vallant!" Jimper's voice piped. "We are saved!"

Vallant opened his mouth to answer and darkness closed in.

CHAPTER TEN

Vallant lay on his back, feeling the gentle breeze that moved against his skin, scenting the perfumed aroma of green, growing things. Somewhere, a bird trilled a melody. He opened his eyes, looked up at a deep blue sky in which small white clouds sailed, row on row, like fairy yachts bound for some unimaginable regatta. All around were small sounds like the peeping of new-hatched chicks. He turned his head, saw a gay toy pavilion of red-and-white striped silk supported by slim poles of polished black wood topped with tiny silver lance-heads. Under it, around it, all across the vivid green of the lawn-like meadow, thronged tiny man-like figures, gaudily dressed, the males with caps and cross-bows, or armed with foot-long swords, their mates in gossamer and the sparkle of tiny gems.

At the center of the gathering, in a chair like a doll's, a corpulent elf lolled in the shadow of the pavilion. He jumped as he saw Vallant's eye upon him. He pointed, peeping excitedly in a strange, rapid tongue. A splendidly armored warrior walked boldly toward Vallant, planted himself by his outflung hand, recited a speech.

"Sorry, Robin Goodfellow," Vallant said weakly. "I don't understand. Where's Jimper?"

The little creature before him looked about, shouted. A bedraggled fellow in muddy brown came up between two armed warriors.

"Alas, Vallant," the prisoner piped. "All is not well in my Land of Galliale."

"Jimper—you look a bit on the unhappy side," Vallant said, "considering you brought off your miracle right on schedule . . ."

"Something's awry, Vallant. There sits my King, Tweeple the Eater of One Hundred Tarts—and he knows not his Ambassador, Jimper!"

"Doesn't know you . . .?" Vallant repeated.

"Jason warned me it would be so," Jimper wailed. "Yet I scarce believed him. None here knows faithful Jimper . . ."

"Are you sure you found the right town? Maybe since you left—"

"Does Jimper not know the place where he was born, where he lived while forty Great Suns came and went?" The mannikin took out a three-inch square of yellow cloth, mopped his forehead. "No Vallant; this is my land—but it lies in the grip of strange enchantments. True, at my call the King sent warriors who guard the cave to kill the Not-men—the Evil Giants—but they would have killed you, too, Vallant, had I not pled your helpless state, and swore you came as a friend. We Sprill-folk have ever feared the memory of the Evil Giants."

"Kill me?" Vallant started to laugh, then remembered the shafts bristling in the bodies of the Niss. "I've come too far to get myself killed now."

"Near you were to a longer journey still, Vallant. I know not how long the King will stay his hand."

"Where are we, Jimper? How did we get here?"

"The king's men dragged you here on a mat of reeds."

"But—how did we get out of the cave . . .?"

"Through the Portal, Vallant—as I said, yet you would not believe!"

"I'm converted," Vallant said. "I'm here—wherever here is. But I seem to remember a job of world-saving I was supposed to do."

Jimper looked stricken. "Alas, Vallant! King Tweeple knows naught of these great matters! It was he whom Jason told of the Great Affairs beyond the Portal, and the part the Folk must play."

"So I'm out of a job?" Vallant lay for a moment, feeling the throb in his head, the ache that spread all through his shoulder and back.

"Maybe I'm dreaming," he said aloud. He made a move to sit up—

"No, Vallant! Move not, on your life!" Jimper shouted. "The King's archers stand with drawn bows if you should rise to threaten them!"

2

Vallant turned his head; a phalanx of tiny bowmen stood, arrows aimed, a bristling wall of foottall killers. Far away, beyond the green meadow, the clustered walls and towers of a miniature city clung to a hillside. Jimper stood steadfastly by, looking worried.

"Didn't you tell the King I came to help him?" Vallant called.

"I pledged my life on it, Vallant" the little man replied fervently, "but he names me stranger. At last he agreed that so long as you lay sorely hurt, no harm could come of you—but take care! The King need but say the word, and you are lost, Vallant!"

"I can't lie here forever, Jimper. What if it rains?"

"They prepare a pavilion for you, Vallant—but first must we prove your friendship." Jimper mopped his face again. Vallant stared up at the sky.

"How badly am I hurt?" Vallant moved slightly, testing his muscles. "I don't even remember being hit."

"A near-miss, meant to warn you, Vallant—but

great stone chips are buried in your flesh. The King's surgeons could remove them—if he would so instruct them. Patience now, Vallant; I will treat with him again.''

Vallant nodded, watched as Jimper, flanked by his guards, marched back to kneel before the pudgy ruler. More piping talk ensued. Then Jimper returned, this time with two companions in crumpled conical hats.

''These are the royal surgeons, Vallant,'' he called. ''They will remove the flints from your back. You have the royal leave to turn over—but take care; do not alarm him with sudden movements.''

Vallant complied, groaning at the until now unnoticed ache in his back. He felt a touch, twisted his head to see a two-foot ladder lean against his side. A small face came into view at the top, apprehensive under a pointed hat. Vallant made what he hoped was an encouraging smile.

''Good morning, doctor,'' he said. ''I guess you feel like a sailor getting ready to skin a whale . . . .'' Then he fainted.

CHAPTER ELEVEN

Vallant sat on a rough log bench, staring across the eighteen-inch stockade behind which he had been fenced for three weeks now—as closely as he could estimate time, in a land where the sun stood overhead while he slept, wakened, and slept again. Now it was behind the tops of the towering, poplar-like trees, and long shadows lay across the lawns under a sky of green and violet and flame. A mile away, lights glittered from a thousand tiny windows in the toy city of Galliale.

"If I could but convince the King," Jimper piped dolefully, a woebegone expression on his pinched features. "But fearful is the heart of Tweeple; not like the warrior kings of old, who slew the Evil Giants."

"These Evil Giants—were they the Niss?"

"Well might it be, Vallant. The legends tell that they were ugly as trolls and evil beyond the imagining of man or Sprill. Ah, but those were brave days, when the Great Giants had fallen, and only the Folk fought on."

"Jimper, do you suppose there's any truth in these legends of yours?"

The tiny mannikin stared. "Truth? True they be as carven stone, Vallant! True as the bolt sped from the bow! Look there!'' He pointed to a gaunt stone structure rising from a twilit hill beyond the forest to the east.

"Is that a dream? But look at the great stones of it! Plain it is that Giants raised it once, long and long ago."

"What is it?"

"The Tower of the Forgotten; the legend tells that in it lies a treasure so precious that for it a King would give his crown; but the Thing of Fear, the Scaled One, the Dread Haik set to guard it by the Evil Giants, wards it well, pent in the walls."

"Oh, a dragon, too. I must say you have a completely equipped mythology, Jimper. What about these Great Giants—I take it they were friendly with the Sprill?"

"Great were the Illimpi, Vallant, and proud were the Sprill to serve them. But now they are dead, vanished all away; and yet, some say they live on, in their distant place, closed away from their faithful Folk by spells of magic, and the Scaled Haik of the Niss."

"Jimper—you don't believe in magic?"

"Do I not? Have not I, and you as well, seen the Cave of No Return with our own eyes—and worse, passed through it?"

"That's the tunnel we came in by, Jimper. You went through it with your friend Jason on the way out—and now you've returned."

"Ah, have I indeed, Vallant? True it is I passed through the Cave—and only my sworn fealty to my King forced me to it—but have I returned in truth? Who is there who welcomes my return?"

"I admit that's a puzzler . . ." Vallant conceded.

"But what about the squad of archers who met us?"

"They stopped short of the Portal, Vallant. Only their swift arrows crossed over; and the Portal affects only living beings, and such articles as touch them."

"It's one for the philosophers," Vallant said sympathetically. "But let's just accept that part for now, and figure out what we're going to do; the Niss may come storming in through the Cave any time, you know. And beam-guns against crossbows are bound to win."

"That we need not fear, Vallant," Jimper piped. "The Not-men fear the Cave from which none returns—as well they might. But we are still in peril, Vallant; yet does the King ponder our fate. He is sore troubled, and not without reason."

"The Portal must be some sort of high-tech gadget. I wonder what it's for?"

"Tales have I heard of others, long ago, who came from the cave, strangers to the Tribe of Sprill—and yet of our blood and customs. Always they talked of events unknown, and swore they had but ventured out into the Blue Ice—and now I am of their number; the stranger in his own land, whom no one knows."

Vallant raised his head, then his torso, to rest on one elbow so as to see over the wall. Far beyond the lawn, he saw a procession on the winding road which descended from the foothills beyond the town. It advanced slowly, led by torchbearers. Midway along the column Vallant made out the shape of an animal-drawn open vehicle.

"What's that?" he asked his tiny companion.

Jimper jumped high to catch a glimpse over the mighty foot-and-a-half-high barrier.

"The royal coach," he said excitedly. "Either our gracious Queen, or her fair daughter, the Princess Touch-me-not." He looked up at Vallant, his face lit by some inner fire. "Fair is she as the Spring dawn, Vallant. But headstrong, they say. Else never would the King permit her so to draw nigh to danger."

Vallant nodded, watching as the procession approached a long trestle bridge spanning the deep ravine through which the river flowed; his eyes strayed upstream, where his attention was caught by the slow movement of an ancient tree high on an undercut bluff above the rushing waters. It was leaning toward the precipice, farther, then suddenly toppling as the soil beneath it crumbled away. Roots bare, the great tree fell with dreamlike grace, down, down, to impact in a mighty splash, to be swept downstream at once.

Vallant caught up Jimper, pointed. "When that hits the bridge—" he blurted. "Somebody has to warn them back!"

"Too late, Vallant," Jimper said. "See, even now they cross." Now Vallant saw a stir among the King's men, much too far from the bridge to help.

"Excuse me, partner," Vallant said, putting Jimper carefully on the ground. "I think I'd better get moving." He stepped over the wall, took a few careful steps as the crowd scattered before him, then broke into a run.

He felt a sharp pain like a bee-sting in his left calf, but only redoubled his pace, past the pavilion, across the green-fuzzed lawn, skirting the edge of the town, up a slope—and topping the rise, saw the bridge below, just as the current bore the immense battering-ram of the fallen tree against the spidery log truss-work, which buckled, splintered one-inch logs flying outward. The road-bed sagged. The advance guard of the parade had halted, and now turned and ran—not for safety, but for the carriage, where they swarmed, gripping the wheel-rims, planting their small bodies in its path as the draft-beasts reared and plunged. The animals were as big as small dogs, Vallant judged, and somewhat resembled the extinct *eohippus*. Terrified, the nervous beasts fought the Sprill who would halt the royal phaeton. In spite of all their efforts, the ornately decorated vehicle rolled through the press, leaving more than one small figure inert behind it. Now on the downslope toward the break, where the uprearing branches of the tree loomed gigantic, it gathered speed. In it, two terrified Sprillwomen clutched each other, one stout and matronly, the other slim and golden-haired. Vallant pelted downslope at full speed, paused only for an instant at the grassy bank. A few yards away, the bridge was breaking up as the swift current forced the tree against and under it. Vallant splashed into the foot-deep, icy waters, fending off flying twigs and splinters, caught the sagging structure, and thrust it back. Now under the bridge, he bent his knees, fitted his shoulders under the main beams of the central span, braced himself and heaved. Almost, the weight of timber was too much, but at last Vallant felt it yield, rising back near its original position. Once, his foot slipped, and he lost ground for a moment, but was able to re-seat his shoulders, and stabilize the collapsing span. Above the roar of the turbu-

lent stream, he heard the splintering of wood and
the shrill cries of the Sprill folk on the bridge.
With an effort, he was able to raise his head far
enough to see the roadway, where the carriage was
sliding sideways toward the ragged break in the
timber span, the little 'horses' scrabbling with three-
toed feet for footing. In the open vehicle, the stout
woman in black cowered in her seat, her hands
over her face, but the slim princess sat upright, her
piquant face calm beneath her unruffled, blonde
coiffure on which jewels sparkled like morning
dew on the grass. Vallant reached up, braced a
hand against the road-bed, and pushed hard enough
nearly to thrust himself backward, but the bridge
yielded, reluctantly closing the gap, and arresting
the fatal slide of the state carriage toward the edge.
The animals regained their equilibrium, and quickly
hauled their burden across the splintered section,
into the clear span beyond. Vallant was tiring
rapidly. He held on, watching, as the procession
resumed its progress, as the carriage rolled off
onto the stone roadbed and beyond the final buttress,
the excited entourage trailing closely. Then, at
last, he ducked and stepped clear, as the bridge,
with a final crashing and rending of great, wrist-
thick logs, collapsed into the river, and the shattered tree moved on downstream in a clotted mass of
broken wood. Spent, he staggered a few steps and
fell headlong.

2

Vallant awoke to a dull throbbing in his lower leg; he groped, encountered a quarter-inch wooden peg standing in the flesh of his calf. Barely enough of the six-inch length of the crossbow bolt projected to afford a grip. He pulled it out with a quick jerk, held it before his face, and reflected that it was well that the polished brass head was unbarbed. A gasp of astonishment had sounded in unison from the throng of Sprill folk surrounding him. Near at hand Jimper was in earnest conversation with the conical-hatted royal surgeons. He hurried to Vallant's head.

"Well done, Vallant! Now are you a hero indeed to the populace, though no word of commendation has yet come from the King, whose command to move not you so dramatically defied! Still, that is a trifle compared to the rescue of the Princess Touch-me-not!"

3

Vallant rose, looking across toward the city. A long procession of torch-bearers was filing from the city gates, winding across the dark plain toward Vallant's stockade. "It looks as though we have more visitors coming, Jimper."

"Woe, Vallant! This means the King has decided your fate! Well has he wined this night—and drink was never known to temper the mercy of the King!"

"If they're coming here to fill me full of arrows, I'm leaving!"

"Wait, Vallant! The captain of the guard is a decent fellow; I'll go to meet them. If they mean you ill, I'll . . . I'll snatch a torch and wave it thus . . ." Jimper made circular motions above his head.

Vallant nodded. "Ok, partner—but don't get yourself in trouble."

Half an hour later, the calvalcade halted before Vallant, Jimper striding beside the breast-plated Captain. He ran forward. "Mixed news, Vallant; this is the judgment of the King: that you have done a mighty service to the Sprill-folk; but he requires further proof of your good-will."

"If I fail?" Vallant prompted.

"Then you shall enter the Cave of No Return, whence no man or Sprill has ever come back."

4

The main avenue of the city of Galliale was ten feet wide, cobbled with cut stones no bigger than dice, winding steeply up between close-crowded houses, some half-timbered, others of intricately patterned masonry, with tiny shops below, gay with lights and merchandise, and open casement windows above, from which small, sharp-nosed faces thrust, staring at the looming giant who strode along, surrounded by the helmeted knee-high warriors of the King, toward the dazzling tower of light that was the Royal Palace of Tweeple the Eater of One Hundred Tarts.

"I don't understand why his Highness isn't content to let me sit out there under my canopy and smell the flowers," Vallant said to Jimper, who rode on his shoulder. "I've even volunteered to be his royal bodyguard—"

"He sees you grow well and strong, Vallant. He fears you may yet turn on the Folk as did the Evil Giants in the olden time."

"Doesn't the dramatic incident of the bridge convince him I'm the good variety?" Vallant persisted. "I'd be handy to have around if that Niss who escaped came back, with a couple of his friends."

"Never will he return, Vallant! All who enter the Cave—"

"I know—but if he sends *me* out there in the cold, I'm likely to turn around and sneak right back in—tradition or no."

"Ah, if Jason were but here to vouch for you," Jimper piped. "Well he knew the tongue of the Sprill, and wondrous the tales he told; charmed was King Tweeple, and many were the honors of Jason, the Giant. But now, alas, the King knows naught of all these things."

"How did Jason happen to find Galliale?"

"He told of a great battle fought between the worlds, where Niss died like moths in the flame under the mighty weapons of the men of Earth—"

"The old man talked to me about a war; he said we lost. Anyway, we never built any warships."

"Jason's ship was hurt," Jimper went on. "He fell far, far, but at last brought the ship to ground among the Blue Ice crags. He saw the Portal among the snows—the same in which we fought the Notmen, Vallant—and so he came to fair Galliale."

"And then he left again—"

"But not until he had tarried long and long among us, Vallant. At his wish, sentinels were posted, day and night, to watch through the Cave of No Return, which gives a fair view of the icy slopes and the plain beyond, for sight of men. Often, when he had drunk a hogshead or two of the King's best ale, he would groan, and cry aloud to know how it went with the battle of the Giants; but he knew the magic of the Cave, and so he waited. And then one day, when he had grown old and bent, the sentries gave him tidings that a strange vessel lay in view beyond the Cave. Grieved was the King, and he swore that he would set his bowmen to guard the entrance to that enchanted path, that Jason the Teller of Tales might not walk down it to be seen no more; but Jason only smiled and said that go he would, asking only that an Ambassador be sent with him, to treat with the Giants; and it was I, Jimper, warrior and scholar, whom the King chose.''

5

"That was quite an honor," Vallant replied gravely. "Too bad he doesn't remember it; and I'm sorry I don't know any stories I could charm the old boy with. I haven't made much headway with the language yet."

"Long before Jason there was another Giant who came to Galliale," Jimper chirped. "No talker was he, but a mighty Giant of valor. The tale tells how he went in against the Scaled One, to prove his love to the King of those times. I heard the tale from my grandfather's father, when I was but a fingerling, when we sat in a ring under the moon and talked of olden times. He came from the Cave—hurt, as you were, Vallant. And the King of those times would have slain him—but in sign of friendship, he entered the Tower of the Forgotten, there to battle the Fanged One who guards the treasures. Then did the King know that he was friend indeed, and of the race of goodly Giants—''

''And what happened to him in the end?''

''Alas, never did he return from the Tower, Vallant—but honored was his memory!''

The procession had halted in the twenty-foot Grand Plaza before the palace gates. The warriors formed up in two ranks, flanking Vallant, bows ready. Beyond a foot-high, spike-topped wall, past a courtyard of polished stones as big as dominoes, the great two-foot high entrance to the palace blazed with light. Beyond it, Vallant caught a glimpse of intricately carved paneling, tiny-patterned tapestries, and a group of Sprill courtiers in splendid costumes, bowing and curtsying as the plump elf-king waddled forth to stand, hands on hips, staring boldly up at Vallant.

He spoke in a shrill voice, waving ringed hands, pausing now and again to quaff a thimble-sized goblet offered by a tiny Sprill lad no taller than a chipmunk.

He finished, and a servant handed him a scarlet towel to dry his pink face. Jimper, who had climbed down and taken up a position in the row of Sprill beside the King, came across to Vallant.

''The King says . . .'' He paused, swallowed. ''That his royal will is . . .''

''Go ahead,'' Vallant urged, eyeing the ranks of ready bowmen. ''Tell me the worst.''

''To prove your friendship, Vallant—you must enter the Tower of the Forgotten, and there slay the Fanged One, the Scaled One, the Eater of Fire!''

Vallant let out a long sigh. ''You had me worried there for a minute, Jimper," he said, almost gaily. "I thought I was going to provide a target for the royal artillery—"

"Jest not, Vallant!" Jimper stamped angrily. "Worse by far is the fate decreed by the King! Minded am I to tell him so—"

"Don't get yourself in hot water, Jimper: it's OK. I'm satisfied with the assignment."

"But, Vallant! No one—not even a Great Giant— can stand against the Fearsome One whom the Evil Giants set to guard the tower!"

"Will he be satisfied if I go into the Tower and come out again alive—even if I don't find the dragon?"

"Delude yourself no more, Vallant! The Scaled One waits there—"

"Still—"

"Yes, to enter the Tower is enough. But—"

"Fair enough. I may not come out dragging the monster by the tail, but the legend won't survive the experiment. When do I go?"

"As soon as may be . . ." Jimper shuddered, then drew himself erect. "But have no fear, Vallant; Jimper will be at your side."

Vallant smiled down at the tiny warrior.

"That's a mighty brave thing to do, Jimper," he said seriously. "I wish I could put your mind at rest about the dragon."

Jimper looked up at him, hands on hips. "And I, Vallant, wish that I could stir in you some healthful fear." He turned, strode back across the courtyard to the King, saluted, spoke briefly. A murmur ran out from the group of courtiers; then a treble cheer went up, while tiny caps whirled high. The King signalled, and white-clad servitors surged forward, setting up tables, laying out heaped platters, rolling great one-pint hogsheads into position.

"The King decrees a night of feasting, Vallant!" Jimper chirped, running to him. "And you too shall dine!"

Vallant watched while a platform normally used for speeches was set up and vivid rugs as fine as silk were laid out on it; then he seated himself and accepted a barrel of ale, raised it in a toast to the King.

"Eat, drink, and be merry . . ." he called.

"If you can," Jimper said, mournful again, "knowing what tomorrow will bring."

CHAPTER TWELVE

In the fresh light of morning, Vallant strode across the emerald velveteen of the Plain of Galliale, feeling the cool air in his face, ignoring the throb in his head occasioned by last night's five barrels of royal ale, watching the silhouette of the tower ahead growing larger against the dawn sky. A long sword—a man-sized duplicate of the tiny one at Jimper's belt—brought from the King's treasury of Ancient Things for his use, swung at his side; in his hand he carried a nine-foot spear with a head of polished brass. Behind him trotted a full battalion of the Royal Guard, lances at the ready.

"I'll have to admit that King Tweeple went all-out in support of the expedition, Jimper," Vallant said. "Even if he did claim he'd never heard of your friendly giant."

"Strange are the days when valued tales of old are unknown to the King. But no matter—pleased is he to find a champion."

"Well, I hope he's just as pleased when I come out and report that the Scaled One wasn't there after all."

Jimper looked up from where he scampered at Vallant's side. He was splendid now in a new scarlet cloak and a pink cap with a black plume.

"Vallant, the Scaled One dwells in the Tower; as sure as blossoms bloom and Kings die!"

Another quarter hour's walk brought Vallant and his escort through the forest of great six-foot conifers and out onto a wild-grown slope where long mounds overgrown with vines and brambles surrounded the monolithic tower at its crest. Near at hand a slab of white stone gleamed through the underbrush. Vallant went closer and pulled the growth away to reveal a weathered man-sized bench-top.

"Hey, it looks as though someone used to live here—and a giant at that." He glanced at the tumuli, some large, some small, forming an intersecting geometric pattern that reached up to the Tower's base.

"Those are the ruins of buildings, and walls," he guessed. "This whole hill-top was built up at one time—a long time ago."

"Once the Castle of those Giants whom the Sprill served rose in splendor here," Jimper piped. "Then the Evil Giants came and threw down its towers and slew our masters with weapons of fire; there was a great King among the Sprill in those days, Vallant: Josro the Sealer of Gates. He it was who led the folk in the war against the Ugly Ones." He looked up at the Tower. "But, alas, the invulnerable Scaled One lives on to wall away the treasure of the Illimpi."

"Well, let's see if we can go finish the job, Jimper." Vallant went up past the mounded ruins. At the top he paused, looking back down the silent slope. "It must have been beautiful once, Jimper," he said. "A palace of white marble, and the view all across the valley . . ."

"Fair it was, and enchanted is its memory," Jimper said. "Long have we feared this place, but now we come to face its dreads. Lead on, Vallant; Jimper is at your side!"

A shrill trumpet note pierced the air. The troop of King's Lancers had halted. Their captain called an order; the two-foot lances swung down in a salute.

"They wait here," Jimper said. "The King will not risk them closer—and they guard our retreat, if the Scaled One should break out, which Fate forfend!"

Vallant returned the salute with a wave of his hand. "I guess if you believe in dragons, to come this far is pretty daring." He glanced down at Jimper. "That makes you a regular hero, partner."

"And what of you, Vallant? In your vast shadow Jimper walks boldly, but you go with only your lance and blade to meet the Terrible One!"

"That doesn't count; I don't really expect to meet him."

2

Now four warriors came forward, stumbling under the weight of a foot-long box slung from their shoulders by leather straps. They lowered it gingerly before Vallant, scampered back to the ranks.

"What's this, a medal—already?" Vallant pressed a stud on the side of the flat box; its lid popped up. Nestled in a fitted case lay a heavy electro-key of unfamiliar design. Vallant picked it up, whistled in surprise.

"Where did this come from, Jimper?"

"When long ago the Sprill-folk slew the Evil Ones, this did they find among the spoils. Long have we guarded it, until our goodly Giants should come again."

Vallant examined the heavy key. "This is a beautiful job of microtronic engineering, Jimper. And it must date back to primitive times on Terra. I'm beginning to wonder who these Giants of yours were." He went up the last few yards of the vine-grown slope to the vast man-sized door of smooth, dark material which loomed up in the side of the Tower; the structure itself, Vallant saw, was not of stone, but of a weathered synthetic, porous and discolored with age.

"I'd give a lot to know who built this, Jimper," he said. "It must have been a highly technical people; that stuff looks like it's been there for a lot of years."

"Great were our Giants, and great was their fall. Long have we waited their return. Now it may be that you, Vallant, and Jason, are the first of those ancient ones to come back to your Galliale."

" 'Fraid not, Jimper. But we can still be friends." Vallant studied the edge of the door.

"Looks like we'll have to dig, Jimper. The dirt's packed in here, no telling how deep." Jimper unsheathed his eight-inch sword, handed it to Vallant. "Use this; a nobler task could not be found for it."

Vallant set to work. Behind him, the ranks of the bowmen stood firm, watching. The unyielding surface of the door extended down six inches, a foot, two feet, before he came to its lower edge.

"We've got a job ahead, partner," Vallant said. "I hope this snoozing dragon of yours is worth all the effort."

"For my part," Jimper said. "I hope the sound of our digging awakens him not too soon."

3

Two hours later, with the door cleared of the packed soil and an arc excavated to accommodate its swing, Vallant returned Jimper's sword, then took the key from the box.

"Let's hope it still works; I'd hate to try to batter my way past that . . ." He lifted the key to the slot in the locking bar; there was a deep-seated *click!*, a rumble of old gears.

"It looks as though we're in business," Vallant said and hammered back the heavy rough-hewn beam that had secured the massive door from the outside; then, levering with his swordblade, he swung the thick panel back, looked into a wide corridor inches deep in dust. The Captain of the Guard and four archers came up, waiting nervously to close the door as soon as Vallant was safely inside. Jimper sneezed. Vallant stooped, lifted him to his shoulder. He waved to the escort, who raised a nervous cheer, then stepped into the dust of the corridor, watched as the door slowly clanked shut behind him.

"We're in, Jimper," he said. "Now—which way to the dragon?"

Jimper fingered his cross-bow, staring ahead along the dim hall. "H-he could be anywhere . . ."

"Let's take a look around." Vallant explored the length of the corridor which circled the Tower against the outer wall, floundering through dust drifted deep under the loopholes high in the walls. At one point a great heap almost blocked the passage. He kicked at it, yelped; rusted metal plates showed, where the covering of dust was disturbed.

"It looks like a dump for old armor," he complained, clambering over the six-foot obstruction. "Maybe this was an early junk-yard. . . ."

Jimper muttered fretfully, "Walk softly, Vallant. . . ."

They completed the circuit, then took a stairway, mounted to a similar passage at a higher level. Everywhere the mantle of dust lay undisturbed. They found rooms, empty except for small metal objects of unfamiliar shape, half buried in the dust. Once Vallant stooped, picked up a statuette of bright yellow metal.

"Look at this, Jimper," he said. "It's a human figure . . .!"

"True," Jimper agreed, squinting at the three-inch image. "No Sprill form is that."

"This place must have been built by men, Jimper!

Or by something so like them that the differences don't show. And yet, we've only had space travel for a few decades—''

"Long have the Giants roamed the worlds, Vallant.''

"Maybe—but we humans have been Earth-bound until just lately. It's comforting to know that there are other creatures somewhere that look something like us—I guess.''

4

They followed corridors, mounted stairs, prowled through chambers large and small. Faint light from tiny apertures in the walls was the only illumination. High in the Tower, they came to a final, narrow flight of steps. Vallant looked up.

"Well,'' he said dubiously "if he's not up here, I think we can consider the mission accomplished.''

"Certain it is that somewhere lurks the Dread One,'' Jimper chirped. "Now l-let him b-beware!''

"That's the spirit.'' Vallant went up the stairs—gripping his sword now in spite of his skepticism; if there were anything alive in the Tower, it would have to be here . . .

He emerged in a wide, circular room, high-vaulted, thick with dust. A lustrous cube, white, frosty-surfaced, dust-free, twelve feet on a side, was mounted two feet clear of the floor at the exact center of the chamber. It seemed almost to glow in the dim room. Cautiously, Vallant circled it. The four sides were identical, unadorned, shimmering white.

Vallant let his breath out, sheathed the sword. "That's that," he said. "No dragon."

Perched on his shoulder, Jimper clutched his neck.

"I fear this place, Vallant," he piped. "We have blundered—I know not how . . ."

"We're all right, old timer," Vallant soothed. "Let's take a look around. Maybe we can pick up a souvenir to take back to old Tweepie—"

"Vallant, speak not with disrespect of my King!" Jimper commanded.

"Sorry." Vallant's boots went in to the ankle as he crossed the drifted floor to the glistening polyhedron; he touched its surface; it was cool, slippery as graphite.

"Funny stuff," he said. "I wonder what it's for?"

"Vallant, let us not linger here."

Vallant turned, looked around the gloomy room. Vague shapes bulked under the dust blanket. He went to a tablelike structure, blew at it, raising a cloud that made Jimper sneeze. He brushed at the array of dials and bright-colored knobs and buttons that emerged from the silt.

"It's some kind of control console, Jimper! What do you suppose it controls?"

"L-let us depart, Vallant!" Jimper squeaked. "I like not these ancient rooms!"

"I'll bet it has something to do with *that* . . ." Vallant nodded toward the cube. "Maybe if I push a couple of buttons—'' He jabbed a finger at a large scarlet lever in the center of the panel. It clicked down decisively.

"Vallant—meddle not with these mysteries!" Jimper screeched. He crouched on Vallant's shoulder, eyes fixed on the lever.

"Nothing happened," Vallant said. "I guess it was too much to expect . . ." He paused. A draft stirred in the room; dust shifted, moving on the table-top.

"Hey—" Vallant started.

Jimper huddled against his neck, moaning. Dust was flowing across the floor, drifting toward the glossy surface of the cube, whipping against it— and beyond. Vallant felt the draft increase, fluttering the fabric of his ship-suit. The dust was rising up in a blinding cloud now; Vallant ducked his head, started toward the door. The wind rose to whirlwind proportions, hurling him against the wall; air was whining in through the loopholes; dust whipped and streamed, flowing to the face of the cube, which glared through the obscuring veil now with a cold, white light. Vallant lunged again for the door, met a blast like a sand-storm that sent him reeling, Jimper still clinging to his perch. He struggled to a sheltered angle between floor and wall, watched as the wind whirled the dust away, scouring the floor clean, exposing a litter of metallic objects and human bones, and one skeletal, mummified Niss. Nearby lay a finger-ring, an ornate badge, an odd-shaped object that might have been a hand-gun. Beyond were a scatter of polished metal bits, the size and shape of shark teeth.

Now, suddenly, the wind was lessening. The white-glaring rectangle was like an open window with a view of a noon-day fog. The last swirls of

dust flashed toward it and were gone. The shrilling
of the gale died. The room was still again.

"Now must we flee . . ." Jimper whistled; he
flapped dust from his cloak, settled his pink cap,
edging toward the door. Vallant got to his feet,
spitting dust. "Not yet, Jimper. Let's take another
look at this . . ." He went close to the glowing
square, stared at it, reached out a hand—

And encountered nothing.

He jerked the hand back quickly.

"Whew! That's cold!" He massaged his numbed
hand. "Half a second and it was stiff!"

Somewhere, far away, a faint, metallic clanking
sounded.

"Vallant! He comes!" Jimper screeched.

"Calm down, Jimper! We're all right. It was a
little thick there for a minute, but I suppose that
was just some sort of equalization process. Or
maybe this thing is a central cleaning device; sort
of a building-sized vacuum cleaner—"

5

Abruptly, the panel before Vallant dimmed.
Shapes whipped across it. The shadowy outlines of
a room appeared, sharpened into vivid focus. Sounds
came through: an electronic hum, the insistent ping-
ing of a bell, then a clump of hurried feet.

A man appeared, stood staring across at Vallant, as through an open doorway.

Or almost a man.

He was tall—near seven feet, and broad through the shoulders. His hair curled close to his head, glossy black as Persian lamb, and through it, the points of two short, blunt horns protruded, not quite symmetrically, on either side of the nobly rounded skull.

He spoke—stacatto words in a language strange to Vallant. His voice was deep, resonant.

"Sorry, sir," Vallant got out, staring. "I'm afraid I don't understand . . ."

The horned man leaned closer. His large dark-blue eyes were fixed on Vallant's.

"Lla," he said commandingly.

Vallant shook his head. He tried a smile; the majestic figure before him was not one which inspired the lighter emotions. "I guess—" he started, then paused to clear his throat. "I guess we've stumbled onto something a little bigger than I expected . . ."

The horned man made an impatient gesture as Vallant paused. He repeated the word he had spoken. Vallant felt a tug at the knee of his suit.

"Vallant!" Jimper peeped. Vallant looked down. "Not now, Jimper—"

"I think—" the mannikin peeped, "I think Jimper understands what the Great Giant means. In the ceremony of the crowning of the King, there is the phrase, 'qa ic lla . . .' It is spoken in the old tongue, the speech of long ago; and the wise elders who were my teachers say those words mean 'when he speaks'! He would have you talk . . ."

The horned giant leaned toward Vallant, as though

to see below the edge of the invisible plane between them. Vallant stooped, raised Jimper up
chest-high. The mannikin straightened himself; then,
standing on Vallant's hand, he doffed his feathered
cap, bent nearly double in a deep bow.

"*Ta p'ic ih sya, Illimpi*," he chirped.

A remarkable change came over the horned man's
face. His eyes widened; his mouth opened—then a
vast smile lit his face like a floodlight.

"*I'Ipliti!*" he roared. He turned, did something
out of sight of Vallant beyond the edge of the
cube, whirled back. He spoke rapidly to Jimper.
The little creature replied, and Vallant heard his
name spoken as Jimper indicated him with a courtly
gesture. The horned man spoke again, commandingly. In reply, Jimper spread his hands, looking
contrite.

"*N'iqi*," he said. "*Niqi, Illimpi.*"

The giant nodded quickly, looked keenly at
Vallant.

"Lla, Vallant," he commanded.

"He knows my name . . ." Vallant gulped.
"What am I supposed to talk about?"

"He is a Great Giant," Jimper peeped excitedly.
"Well he knows Jimper's kind, from of old. Tell
him all, Vallant—all that has befallen the race of
Giants since last the Portal closed."

CHAPTER THIRTEEN

Vallant talked for five minutes, while the giant beyond the invisible barrier adjusted controls out of sight below the Portal's edge.

". . . when I came to, I was here—"

The Giant nodded suddenly. "Well enough," he said clearly. Vallant stared in surprise. The horned man's lips, he noticed, did not move in synchronization with his words.

"Now," the Giant said, "what world are you?"

"What . . . how . . .?" Vallant started.

"A translating device; I am Cessus the Communicator. What world are you?"

"Well, I would have said I was on Pluto, except that . . . I couldn't be. And on the other hand, I must be . . ."

"Your language . . . a strange tongue it is; none that I have known in my days in the Nex. Best I find you on the Locator . . ." He flipped unseen levers; his eyes widened.

"Can it be?" He stared at Vallant. "A light glows on my panel that has not been lit these ten Grand Eons . . . that of Lost Galliale . . ."

Vallant nodded eagerly. "That's right—Galliale is what Jimper calls the place. But—"

"And your people; are all—as you?"

174

"More or less."

"None have these?" He pointed.

"Horns? No. And this isn't my home world, of course. I come from Terra—third from the Sun."

"But—what of the Illimpi of Galliale?" The Giant's face was taut with strain.

"Nobody lives here but Jimper's people. Right, Jimper?"

"True," Jimper spoke up, "once the Evil Giants—foes of the Great Giants—came; but from thicket and burrow we crept, after the last Great Giant fell. We loosed our bolts to find their marks in vile, green hide, then slipped away to fight again. So we dealt with them all, we bowmen, for against our secret bolts, of what avail their clumsy lightnings? The last of them fled away down the Cave of No Return, and free at last was my Land of Galliale from their loathsome kind. Now long have we waited for our Giants to come back; and we have tilled and spun and kept fair the land."

"Well done, small warrior," Cessus said. He studied Vallant's face. "You are akin to us—that much is plain to see; and you say you dwell on the double world that lies third from the Sun—so some few survivors made good their secret flight there—"

"Survivors of what?"

"Of the onslaught of those evil ones you call the Niss."

"Then—what the old man said was true? They're invaders—"

"That, and more, Vallant! They are the bringers of darkness, the all-evil, the wasters of worlds!"

"But—they haven't wasted the Earth; you hardly notice them; they're just a sort of police force—"

"They are a poison that stains the Galaxy and

devious are their plots. Long ago, they came, destroying—but listen; this was the way of it:

"Ages past, we Illimpi built the Portal—this block of emptiness before which you stand—linking the star-clouds. We sent colonists into the fair new world of Galliale—adventurers, man and woman, the brave ones who never could return; and with them went the Sprill-folk, the faithful Little People.

"They thrived, and in time they built a Gate—a useful link to a sunny world they called Olantea, circling in the fifth orbit of a yellow sun some light-years distant. There they built cities, planted gardens that were a delight to the senses.

Then, without warning, the Niss came to Galliale, they who had long ago been suppressed here in the Home Galaxy; but some few eluded us, pouring through the Gateway, armed with weapons of fire. Swift and terrible was their assault, and deadly the gases they spread abroad, and the crawling vermin to spread their plagues. The peaceful Illimpi of Galliale battled well, and volunteers rushed through the Portal to their aid. But deadly were the weapons of the Niss; they carried the Tower of the Portal and some few, mad with blood-lust, rushed through it, never to return. Then the Portal failed, and lost was our link with our colony. The long centuries have passed, and never did we know till now how it fared with Lost Galliale."

"So the Sprill finished off the Niss, after the Niss had killed the Illimpi?" Vallant summed up. "Nice work, Jimper. But how did you manage it?"

"Proof were we against their sickness," Jimper piped. "But no defense had they against our bows."

"If the Niss are such killers, why haven't they

used their weapons on us? The story the Syndarch
tells is that they're our great friends, sharing their
wisdom—''

"Proof have we seen of that lie," Jimper chirped.
"Deep are the plots of the Niss."

"It is the Portal they seek," Cessus said. "All
who came to Galliale were lost to them. Doubtless
they think to use you."

"Just a minute," Vallant cut in. "I'm lost. The
Niss came through the Gateway from Olantea—
but that was held by the Illimpi. The Niss must
have rebelled and captured the Gateway—which I
take it is some sort of matter transmitter. But why
wasn't Galliale warned? And why is it none of the
Galliales escaped through the Portal here, back to
the home world? And how did the Gateway get
shifted from Olantea to Pluto—''

Cessus was frowning in puzzlement. "Do you
not know, Vallant—''

"Vallant!" Jimper cocked his head. "The Scaled
One—I hear him stir!"

"It's your imagination, Jimper. "We've explored
the whole building, and didn't find him, remember?"

The horned man was looking at Jimper. "What
manner of creature is this Scaled One?"

"It's just a superstition of Jimper's—" Vallant
started.

"A haik, Great Giant," Jimper shrilled. "A
guardian set by the Niss when they had closed the
Portal against the Illimpi, before they fared forth
against the Sprill, from which adventure no Niss
returned—''

Cessus whirled on Vallant. "How have you
restrained the beast?"

Vallant's mouth opened. "I hope you don't mean—" he began—

There was a sudden clangor as of armor clashing against stone.

"The Fanged One comes!" Jimper shrilled.

"What weapon have you?" Cessus rapped out.

"Just this ham-slicer . . ." Vallant gripped the sword-hilt. "But I have a sudden feeling it's not quite what the program requires . . ."

The clatter was louder now; Jimper screeched; the horned Giant whirled to reach behind the screen's edge—

There was a screech of tortured steel from the doorway; a hiss like an ancient steam-whistle split the air. Vallant spun, stared at a vast *thing*—like a jumble of rusted fragments of armor plate, wedged in the doorway, scrabbling with legs like gleaming black cables three inches thick, armed with mirror-bright talons which raked grooves in the hard floor as though it were clay. From a head like a fang-spiked mace, white eyes with pinpoint pupils glared in insane ferocity. The haik surged, sending chips of the door-frame flying as it forced its bulk through the narrow way.

"Ye gods!" Vallant yelled. "Jimper, why didn't you tell me this thing really existed!"

"Tell you I did, Vallant; now slay it with your sword!"

"That pile of junk we climbed over," Vallant said in a shocked tone. "Lucky he's a sound sleeper. I'll do my best, Jimper, but what good is a hat-pin against a man-eating rhino like that!" Vallant backed, watching as the material of the wall chipped and crumbled under the force of the haik's thrust. His eye fell on the gun-like object on

the floor. He jumped for it, caught it up, raised it
and pressed the button on its side. A lance of blue
flame licked out, touched the haik's snout. The
monster clashed its jaws, gained another foot. The
flame played on its cheek, dimmed abruptly, fell
back to a weak yellowish glow, died with a harsh
buzz. Vallant threw the weapon from him.

"Vallant!" Jimper shrieked. "The door-frame!
It crumbles . . .!"

"Sorry, Jimper! I guess we'll just have to round
up a posse and come back after him . . .!" Vallant
grabbed up the little creature, stepped to the screen—

"No, Vallant!" the horned man shouted—

"Here I come, ready or not—" Vallant closed
his eyes, and stepped through the Portal.

CHAPTER FOURTEEN

There was an instant of bitter cold; then silence, a touch of cool air, an odor of almonds . . .

Vallant opened his eyes. A great, dim, vaulted hall arched high above him; far away, mighty columns loomed into shadows. Beyond, an iodine-colored wall towered up, misty with distance, decorated in patterns of black lines set off with glittering flecks of gold and copper.

"Where is he?" Vallant blurted, staring around. "What happened to Cessus the Communicator?"

Jimper huddled against Vallant, peering up into the mists far overhead. "Lost are we now, Vallant. Nevermore will we see the spires of Galliale—nor the drab cities of your world . . ."

"He was right here—and the room behind him . . ."

"Dread are the mysteries of the Great Giants . . ." Jimper keened.

"Well," Vallant laughed shakily. "At least we left the haik behind." He sheathed the unused sword. "I wonder who lives here." Faint echoes rolled back from the distant wall. "We're in a building of some kind; look at this floor, Jimper. Slabs the size of tennis courts. Talk about Giants . . ."

"Vallant—can we not go back? I dread the haik less than I fear this place of echoes."

"Well . . ." Vallant studied the empty air around them. "I don't see anything that looks like a Portal. Maybe if we just feel our way . . ." He took a cautious step, Jimper wriggled down, darted ahead. He paused, puzzled, turned back—and froze, staring. Vallant whirled. At the spot where he had stood, a glossy black cable, dagger tipped, writhed in the air, three feet above the stone floor.

"The haik!" Jimper squealed. With a deafening screech, the many-spiked head of the monster appeared, followed an instant later by its two-ton bulk, crashing thunderously through the Portal. For a moment it crouched as though confused; then at a sound from Jimper, it wheeled with murderous speed on its intended victims.

Vallant whipped out the sword. "Run, Jimper. Maybe I can slow him down for a second or two—"

Jimper snatched the cross-bow from his back, fitted a six-inch quarrel in place, drew and let fly; the dart whistled past Vallant's head, glanced off the haik's armor. The creature gaped tooth-ringed jaws, dug in its talons for the spring—

There was a sudden rush of air, a shriek of wind. From nowhere, a vast grid slammed down, struck with an impact that jarred the floor, knocked Vallant from his feet. He scrambled up, saw the grid receding as rapidly as it had come. The broken thing that had been the haik flicked cable-legs in a last convulsion, then lay, a shattered, rusted hulk, leaking thin fluid against the stone.

"Whatever that was," Vallant said shakily, "it just missed us . . ." He looked up. Far up in the dimness hovered a misty oblong, with small dark patches, whose outline wavered and flowed, bulging and elongating—

Then it withdrew and was gone.

"Jimper . . .!" Vallant croaked. "Did you see that . . .?"

"I saw naught, Vallant," Jimper shrilled. "The haik charged and then—I know not."

"It was . . ." Vallant paused to gulp. "A face . . . a huge, rubbery face, a mile long and five miles up . . . and I'd swear it was looking right at me . . . !"

"*Another invasion of mind-fleas in the Hall,*" said a voice as clear as engraved print.

"*Ill-struck, Brometa,*" a second voice answered. "*I hear their twittering still.*"

"Vallant!" Jimper gasped. "Those there are who speak close by—and in the tongue of the Sprill-folk—yet I see them not . . ."

"N-nonsense," Vallant gulped. "They're speaking English . . . but where are they?"

"*We should have plugged the hole they burrowed last time,*" the silent voice said: "*Here, give me the whisk; I'll attend to these fleas—*"

"No!" Vallant yelled at the top of his lungs, staring upward into the formless shadows. "We're not fleas . . !"

"*Yapud! Did you hear words amid the twitterings just now?*"

There was a pause; distant rumblings sounded.

"*You must have imagined it, Brometa—*"

"*I heard it just as you raised the whisk—*"

"Don't do it!" Vallant bellowed.

"*There! Surely you heard that! It rang in my mind like a light-storm.*"

Staring upward, Vallant saw the vast cloud-face appear again, its shape changing.

"*I see nothing, Yapud.*"

"We're friendly!" Vallant shouted. "Don't swat us!"

"*These fleas have the same irritating way of projecting thought forms out of all proportion to their size—*"

"*More of those hate-scorched vermin who infested the Hall last Great Cycle? Swat them at once!*"

"*No, this is another breed. Those others—Niss, they called themselves—what a vicious mind-stink they raised before we fumigated! Hmmm. This one seems quite different, Yapud.*"

"*Vermin are vermin! Give me the whisk—*"

"*Hold! Little enough I have to divert me here; let me converse awhile with these noisy fleas.*"

"What transpires, Vallant?" Jimper peeped. He gazed worriedly up at Vallant. "Who speaks in Jimper's head?"

"I don't know, Jimper—but it's something that thinks I'm a flea, and doesn't even know about you."

"*Here, you fleas; I'll put a paper on the floor; step upon it, that I may lift you up where I can lay eyes on you.*"

2

There was a great rushing of air. A vast, white shape rushed down, blotting out the mists above. Vallant and Jimper dropped flat, clung to crevices in the floor against the rush of air that whistled past. An immense, foot-thick platform made of compacted bits of rope thudded to the floor fifty feet away, stretching off into the distance. The wind howled and died.

"We're supposed to climb up on that, Jimper," Vallant said. "So they can get a look at us."

"Must we?"

"I guess we'd better—if we don't want to get whisked, like the haik."

Vallant and Jimper got to their feet, walked across to the ragged-edged, spongy mat, clambered up on it. At close range, the fibers that comprised it were clearly visible; it was like a coarse felt of pale straw.

"Ok," Vallant hailed. "Lift away . . ."

They lost their balance as the platform surged up beneath them: a white light appeared, grew. Their direction of motion changed; the paper tilted sickeningly; then, with an abrupt lurch, came to rest. The glare above, like a giant sun, cast blue shadows across the white plain behind them. A mile away, two unmistakable faces loomed, block-long eyes scanning the area, their changing shapes even more alarming at close range.

There it is! A shape like a vast blimp floated into view, pointing.

Yes—and isn't that another one beside it—a hatchling, perhaps?

Ah, poor things; a mother and young. Always have I had a soft spot for maternity.

"Here—" Jimper started.

"Quiet," Vallant hissed. "I'd rather be a live mother than whisked."

"Size is not all," Jimper peeped indignantly.

Now, small ones. Perhaps you'll tell us of your tiny lives—your minuscule affairs, your petty sorrows and triumphs; and who knows? Maybe there'll be a lesson therein for wise T'tun to ponder.

"How can it be that they know the speech of the Sprill?" Jimper chirped.

"They don't—it's some kind of telepathy; it comes through as English, for me."

Here—natter not among yourselves; explain your presence—

Not so harshly, Yapud; you'll frighten the tiny things.

"None so quick to fear are we!" Jimper piped. "Know that we have passed through many strange adventurings, and no enemy yet has seen our heels!"

Ah, this could prove diverting! Start at the beginning, bold mite; tell us all.

"Very well," Jimper chirped. "But at the end of my recital, hopeful I am you'll hold out aid to two poor travelers, lost far from home."

These fleas wish to bargain . . . ?

The offer is fair. Begin.

"When Jason the Giant would leave fair Galliale to seek again his homeland," Jimper chirped, "Jimper was chosen to travel at his side . . ."

3

There was a moment of silence when Jimper, assisted at points by Vallant, had finished his account.

So, the being called Yapud said, *The mind-fleas admit they burrowed a path through our walls—*

A remarkable achievement, for such simple creatures, Brometa said calmly.

Hmmph! I see nothing remarkable in the series of blundering-near-disasters these fleas managed to devise for themselves; why, even a slight exercise of intelligent effort would have aligned their environment correctly—

Yes, Yapud, I've been puzzling over that; and I think I have the answer; these tiny mites dwell in a three-dimensional space—

Spare me your allegorical apologia—

I'm being quite objective, Yapud! These entities— intelligent entities, too, mind you—are confined to a three dimensional frame of reference; obvious

relationships are thus forever beyond their con-
ceptualization.

Vallant and Jimper stood together, watching the
vast faces change and writhe like shapes of smoke
as the creatures conversed.

"Remind them of their promise, Vallant," Jimper
chirped.

Vallant cleared his throat. "Ah . . . now, about
our difficulty; you see—"

You mean, Yapud said, *ignoring him, that they
crawl about, cemented to a three-dimensional space,
like so many Tridographs?"*

*Precisely! As we move, presenting various three-
dimensional views to their gaze, our appearances
must seem to alter quite shockingly. Of course, the
concept of viewing our actual forms in the hyper-
round, from outside, as it were, is quite beyond
them!*

*Poof! You're quite wrong; you've already admit-
ted they tunnelled into the Hall, which certainly
required manipulation in at least four dimensions!*

Hmmm. Another pause. *Ah, I see: the tunnel
was punched through their space by another, more
advanced species; look for yourself, Yapud.*

There was another pause. *Well . . . yes, I see
what you mean . . . odd . . . did you notice the
orientation of the tunnel?*

*No, I hadn't—but now that you mention it, I'm
beginning to see why these poor creatures have
had such a time of it . . .*

"Please, fellows, if you don't mind," Vallant
spoke up. "My friend and I are hoping you'll be
able to help us out; you see, it's very important
that we get back—"

That of course, is out of the question, Yapud

interrupted. *We'll swat these fleas and plug their
tunnel, and then on to other matters . . .*

*Not so fast, my dear Yapud. The energies re-
quired to plug the tunnel would be quite fantastic.
You realize, of course, that it constitutes an infinitely-
repeating nexus series—*

"All this is very interesting, I'm sure," Vallant
put in, "but unfortunately, it's over our heads.
Couldn't you just direct us back to our—uh-tun-
nel—"

*That would do you no good; you'd end in null
space—*

"But it leads to the Tower of the Portal—"

*Surely you understand that since you're travers-
ing a series of tri-valued pseudo-continua, via—
dear me, I'm afraid you won't be able to grasp the
geometry from your unfortunate three-dimensional
viewpoint. But—"*

*Here, Brometa, you're only confusing things.
Place yourself in their frame of reference, as you
suggested yourself a moment ago. Now—*

"But the Portal opened from the Tower; it *has*
to lead back there—" Vallant insisted.

*Tsk, tsk; three-dimensional thinking. No, the
tunnel was devised as a means of instantaneous
travel between points apparently distant to a tri-
dimensional being. Naturally, the energy displaced
by such a transposition required release; thus a
nonentropic vector was established to a locus bear-
ing a temporal relationship to the point of origin
proportional to the value of C.*

"Here," Vallant said desperately. "We're not
getting anywhere. Could I just ask a few questions—
and could you answer in three-D terms?"

Very well. That might be simpler.

"Where are we?"

Ummm. In the Hall of the T'tun, in the Galaxy of Andromeda—and don't say you don't understand; I picked the concepts from your own vocabulary.

Vallant gulped. "Andromeda?"

Correct.

"But we were on Galliale—"

The use of the past tense is hardly correct, since the Portal you used will not be constructed for three million years—in your terms, that is.

"I'm not sure my terms are equal to the job," Vallant said weakly. "How did we happen to get into the past?"

The velocity of light is a limiting value; any apparent exceeding of this velocity must, of course, be compensated for. This is accomplished by the displacement of mass through quarternary space into the past to a distance equal to the time required by light to make the transit. Thus, an 'instantaneous' transit of ten light-years places the traveller ten years in the subjective past, relative to the point of origin—three-dimensionally speaking.

"Ye gods!" Vallant blurted, and swallowed. "Andromeda is over a million light years from Earth; when I went through the Portal, I stepped a million years into the past?"

A million and a half, to be precise.

"But—when the Illimpi came to Galliale through the Portal, they didn't go into the past—or did they?"

Oh, I see; there's a further projection of the tunnel, leading . . . Brometa, how curious! The tunnel actually originates here on the site of the Hall! Just a moment, while I scan through . . .

4

"Vallant," Jimper piped, "what does it all mean?"

"I'm not sure. It seems the Illimpi started from here in Andromeda—and threw a link across to our Galaxy; then they went through, and colonized Galliale—a million and a half years in their past. When I stepped through the Portal, I dumped us another million and a half years back—three million years from Cessus—"

And, of course, Brometa said, *the Gateway between Galliale and Olantea will be a similar link when it is built; it will span merely twenty light-years—*

"Aha!" Vallant exclaimed. "So that's why no one ever comes back from the Cave of No Return, Jimper—they step twenty years into the past when they go out—and another twenty when they come back!"

"Then I came back to Galliale forty years ere I departed?" Jimper squeaked. "Small wonder King Tweeple was leaner, and knew me not . . ."

"But the Niss—the ones that poured through the Gateway into Galliale, back when the Giants were killed off—"

Twenty thousand years ago, Yapud put in.

"Huh? How did you know?" Vallant said surprised.

How? Why I simply examined the data—

Remember, Brometa put in, *your three-valued space places unnatural limitations on your ability to perceive reality. Three-dimensional 'time' is a purely illusory discipline—*

Please, no extended theoretical discourse, Brometa! I'm answering the flea's questions!

"So twenty thousand years ago, the Niss invaded Galliale from Olantea—and dropped twenty years into their past in the process. They couldn't go back, because they'd step out into Olantea, another twenty years earlier—"

—where they promptly expired, as is their custom when surrounded by their enemies, Yapud cut in. *However, on Galliale, they were successful— for a while. When they came, they blazed a path before them with disruptor beams; then they spread plagues which only the Sprill survived.*

"And then the Sprill wiped out the Niss, by hiding and picking them off." Vallant put in. "But . . . The Galliales should have warned the Olanteans; the invasion came from Olantea—twenty years in the future—and they were in communication with the Oleantea of twenty years in the past—"

They had no opportunity; the Niss held the Gateway. On Olantea, the Niss struck with blind ferocity from space; they descended first on the outer Olantean satellite; there they set up an engine with the power to shatter worlds. To save the mother world, the Olanteans launched a desperate assault. They carried the Dome under which the Engine had been assembled, and then, quickly, before they could be overcome, they triggered the energies buried deep in the rock. Thus died the lesser moon of Olantea.

"What about the Niss?"

It was a terrible defeat—but not final. The mighty detonation of the Olantean moon destroyed the equilibrium of the system; vast storms swept the planet; when they ceased, it was seen that Olantea had left its ancient orbit, and drifted now outward and ever outward. Snow covered the gardens and the fountains and the towers of Olantea; the seas froze. A winter came which never Spring would follow.

The Niss—those who remained—struck again—a last, desperate bid to annihilate their enemies. They attacked Olantea, seized the Gateway to Galliale, and poured in their numbers through it, fleeing the cold that now locked Olantea in a mantle of ice. Their fate, you know.

"But what happened to Olantea?"

It found a new orbit at last, far from its Sun. You call it Pluto.

"And the remains of the lost moon are the asteroids," Vallant said, awed. "But—Cessus said that humans were related to the Illimpi . . ."

Some few Illimpi escaped from dying Olantea to colonize the Earth. There they lived in peace for two hundred centuries—until the first flashes of nuclear explosion summoned the Niss via their colony on Mars.

"And now they're occupying us," Vallant said. "Snooping around to find a clue to the Portal . . ."

Bah! That would merely provide us with a plague of the evil nits! Brometa burst out. *That, we can-*

not allow to come to pass. We must give aid to these inoffensive fleas, Yapud—

True, Yapud agreed. *I confess I was quite carried away, viewing the Niss onslaught and the death of a world as I did, from the three-dimensional view-point. I see now that even these mites have feelings of a sort—and the destruction of beauty is a crime, in any continuum!*

"I suppose the old man—" Vallant stopped suddenly. "He came back—from Galliale! That means he came back through time, twenty years—"

Forty years; twenty when he entered Galliale, and twenty more on his departure.

"And he knew! That's why he waited, Jimper! You said he told the King he couldn't leave until the time was right; he posted sentinels by the Gateway to watch the valley of Blue Ice, and settled down to wait. When the Survey Team landed near the Gate, he had his chance!"

"And knowing he would emerge into his past, he brought me with him to prove that he had indeed visited Fair Galliale—"

"But who told him about the Gateway? He—"

"Vallant!" Jimper squeaked. "He came to you, spoke of old days of comradeship, and showed you pictures—"

"Then—that means he *was* Jason—the same Jason I knew!" Vallant shook his head. "But that means I've already—I mean *will* see him again. But how can I get three million years into the future?"

Yes . . . that is something of a problem, Yapud conceded.

"Uh—I know it's asking a lot," Vallant said,

"but if you could just transfer us ahead through time . . ."

No . . . we can scan it—as you visually scan space when you stare into your night sky—but as for travelling in substance—or transmitting three-dimensional beings—

Wait—I have a thought, Brometa put in. *You spoke of the three-dimensional framework; why not . . .* the conversation turned to technicalities.

5

Waiting for the immense beings to conclude their incomprehensible dialog, Vallant and his diminutive ally set out to explore the vast room. First they stepped down from the coarse mat of fibers onto which Brometa had coaxed them for study.

The floor underfoot was of a porous substance resembling a hard synthetic. Far away, at what must have been the end of the gigantic chamber, yellow light flooded in across an open, colonaded terrace. The two intruders walked for hours, Jimper politely refusing Vallant's offer of a ride on his shoulders. At last they reached the open loggia, emerging from semi-darkness into the glare of a big, yellow sun. Far below, for the building they were in seemed to be built on the top of a cliff, a peaceful landscape spread to a curiously distant horizon.

"We're on a world of an unknown sun in another Galaxy," Vallant thought aloud. "Has anyone ever been farther from home than we are?"

"Vallant," Jimper piped. "will I ever see again the towers of Galliale?"

"We'll know as soon as they finish discussing ways and means . . ."

The whisk would be simpler, Yapud was saying, impatiently, when they returned within earshot. *No, I'll do nothing hasty—but what you propose seems unduly to involve us in matters best left to take their course.*

To do nothing would be a crime against ourselves as well as our ancient allies, the Illimpi, Brometa rebuked him.

The Illimpi, Brometa said. *It's just occurred to me that they're remote descendants of ours, Yapud, though, like these fleas, they're bound to a three-dimensional space. We can't allow these Niss-fleas to trouble them.*

Impossible!

But the relationship is quite obvious, once you examine it—

Nonsense! Next you'll be saying these fleas are our kin!

Hmmm. As to that, they appear to be ancestral to the Illimpi—

Nonsense! They're the degenerate descendants of the Illimpi who escaped from freezing Olantea to Earth!

True—but later, they crossed space via mechani-

cal FTL drive, and colonized Andromeda; later, they recolonized the Milky Way via the Portal—

Then it's quite clear! Yapud exclaimed. *I told you the Illimpi were no descendants of ours. These mites are our remotest ancestors!*

Ancestors?

Certainly; they will set up a Portal here, a few years from now, and use it to retransmit themselves to the Milky Way, an additional million and a half years in the past, and from there, they will reestablish a new link to Andromeda, three million years prior to now, and so on, in order to study their past—

"Stop!" Vallant called. "You're making my head ache. Compared to this, the business of Jason and I telling each other about the Gateway is nothing! But how can I start the ball rolling if I'm stranded here?"

Obviously, we can't allow that to happen, Brometa said. *There's no telling what it might do to the probability stress-patterns. But as to how—*

Just a minute, Brometa, Yapud cut in. *Place yourself in their three-valued Universe for a moment; if the transit were made strictly within the parameters of their curious geometry, the aleph and gimel factors would cancel out nicely—*

Why—how obvious! It should have occurred to me, Yapud!

"Have you thought of something?" Vallant asked anxiously.

Fleas, if we place you back in your native spaciotemporal coordinates, will you pledge yourselves to purge your galaxy of Niss? We'll prepare a simple pesticide for you; an elementary excitor effect should be adequate; direct it on a Niss and the creature will blaze up nicely, without affecting other forms of energy concentration. I think a range of one light-year for the hand model should do . . .

I'll attend to preparing a suitable three-dimensional capsule, Yapud put in. *Rather amusing to realize that these fleas can be confined merely by drawing a plane about them* . . . his voice faded.

"What are you going to do?" Vallant asked nervously. "I hope you're keeping in mind that we don't live long enough for any really extended processes . . ."

We'll give you a . . . ah . . . . ship, I think the term is. It will travel at a velocity just under that of electromagnetic radiation—and will follow a route which will require three million years for the transit to your home galaxy. Naturally, the subjective elapsed time aboard will be negligible. The duration of the voyage will be adjusted with precision so as to place you in the close vicinity of Earth at the same time that you departed. We'll take a moment to encapsulate the vessel in certain stress patterns, which will render it impervious to unwelcome interference by the Niss or any others—

With a *whoosh!* of displaced air which sent Vallant and Jimper skittering across the floor, a gleaming, hundred-foot hull swooped down to settle gently a hundred yards away.

I've taken the precaution of installing a duplicator for the production of the anti-Niss weapons, Yapud said; *just set it up in any convenient location and shovel dirt in the hopper at the top—and stand well back from the delivery chute.*

One other detail, Brometa added. *Since the Illimpi will be our ancestors, I think we owe it to them to help all we can. If we nudge Olantea from its cold orbit and guide it back to its ancient position, fifth from the sun, once more it will flower. There seem to be some fifty million Illimpi still there, carefully frozen in special vaults under the ice, awaiting rescue. We can time matters so that they thaw as the Earth-fleas eliminate the last of the Niss.*

That should be a joyous reunion. I note that the first of the new colonists begin to cross to Galliale as soon as the haik follows the fleas here . . .

"What of Jimper?" the Sprill piped. "Long have I fared from the hills of Fair Galliale . . ."

"Don't worry, Jimper," Vallant reassured the little fellow. "I'll drop you off; you'll arrive home another twenty years in your past, but I guess it can't be helped."

Jimper looked startled. "I have but remembered another fanciful tale, told to me long ago, by the father of my grandfather, when he was well gone in strong ale. He told of venturing into the Tower, and travelling far, only to return at last to Galliale . . ."

"The old boy had a tale for every occasion," Vallant said.

"You fail to grasp the implication," Jimper sighed. "For him was I named, Vallant . . ."

Aboard the ship, Vallant slept for a week. When he awoke, Pluto and its big moon hung silver-black in the viewport. He brought the vessel in over the Blue Ice Mountains, settled it by the cave, watched as Jimper scampered to its opening, turned to wave, and disappeared within.

Nine days later, he swept past startled Niss patrols to slide into Earth's atmosphere; one alien vessel which came too near plunged out of control into the Atlantic.

Vallant landed in wooded country north of Granyauck, left the ship by night, caught a ride into the city. On the campus of the University Complex, he found the vast dormitory in which Jason Able was housed, followed numbers until he reached his room. He knocked. The tall, square-jawed redhead opened the door.

"Oh, hi, Ame," he said. "Been on a trip?"

"I guess you could say that. Pour me a beer, Jase, and I'll tell you all about it . . ."

"It seems to me," Able said, after hearing Vallant out, and asking all the urgent questions, "that we don't have to worry. Everything must have worked out all right, or our remote descendants, the T'tun wouldn't have been there, to say nothing of the Illimpi.''

"We can't count on that, Jase," Vallant cautioned. "I think somehow our simple ideas of cause and effect, with cause preceding effect, may be naive. Don't ask me to explain any better than that. I can't. But I think I'd better go with you when you join the Navy tomorrow. I can think of a hundred questions now that I wish I'd asked the old man—you, Jase, forty years on. But I guess it's really better for us not to know the future for sure, trapped in our three-valued space as we are.''

"All right," Able agreed. "I'm glad you're coming with me, Ame. Maybe together we can find a better way to speed up the process of distributing the new anti-Niss weapons.''

"I want to see Galliale again," Vallant said. "I wonder if I can.''

"The Giant stranger who went into the Dread Tower in the legend, and never came out, Ame," Able said soberly. "That was you, I suppose.''

"Right. And Jimper is his own great-great grandpap. So if I go back, it won't be any stranger than what's already in the record.''

THE LONG AND
SHORT OF IT

By
Sandra Miesel

Between them, the Vangard giant and the Galliale pixie measure the breadth of Keith Laumer's talent. These stories are widely separated markers in a span of writing that ranges from farcical comedy to stark tragedy, from whirligig time-travel tales to furious suspense thrillers. But whatever his subject or treatment, Laumer proudly celebrates the triumph of sheer excellence and unswerving will.

Like so many of his stories, "The Other Sky" [1964] ties the space-time continuum in knots as if it were macramé cord. Combining two of Laumer's favorite devices, secret alien conquest and temporal paradox, its mood falls between the seriousness of *Dinosaur Beach* [1971] and the hilarity of *The Great Time Machine Hoax* [1964]. Shifting the scene from a shabby futuristic Earth to a Lilliput pretty enough to please a Victorian fairy painter to an incomprehensible Brobdingnag gives the effect of a lens abruptly changing curvature. This reinforces the plot irony: one race's mortal peril is solved by another's mental ploy.

Far crueler is the irony of "Once There Was a Giant" [1968], that mordant inversion of Jack-the-Giant-Killer. Although benevolent giants are not unknown in European tradition, we commonly regard them as brutish monsters easily vanquished by quick-witted young heroes: "The bigger they come, the harder they fall."

The marvelously realized, wintry planet Vangard, a "sphere of gray cast iron" with a saga-worthy past is a properly Nordic environment. Johnny, the sole inhabitant of this Jotunheim resembles a frost giant, the Norse personification of cold. But he also displays the best qualities of the fearsome giant-slaying god Thor, "the very apotheosis of the warrior, rude, simple, and noble, always ready to face combat and danger, a tireless adversary of giants and demons, a hero without fear, who disdained repose." His surname "Thunder" is equivalent to "Donar," Thor's Germanic counterpart. Johnny's fate also suggests the Norse myth of Ymir, the primordial ice-born giant whom three gods slew and from whose corpse the world was made. The Vangard native must die so that a race of lesser stature—in every sense of the term—can possess his planet. But here the murder will lead to destruction, not creation.

Laumer builds reversals directly into the fabric of this story. He makes the villain his first-person protagonist—an unusual literary ploy for this author. Watching events through the betrayer's narrow eyes enlarges his innocent prey, spiritually as well as physically. In the perfection of his malice, Ulrik the evil-doer is a total mockery of the typical Laumer hero. His skill and dedication are directed to vicious ends. His alias borrows the revered names of an emperor and a general. His cover story exploits the valiant ideals of his victim.

Ulrik's falseness only makes Johnny more true—

light shines brighter against darkness. He lives out
the fidelity his tomentor only feigns. Compare his
constancy with that of Jim Carnaby in "Thunderhead" [1963]. There, an ageing space officer climbs
to his death on a frozen mountain in fulfillment of
a duty everyone around him thinks meaningless.
Carnaby's sacrifice stops an alien invasion but
Johnny's victory is solely moral. His heroism is
known to but one man—his murderer.

No desire for fame or glory drives Johnny to his
goal. [His romanticized posthumous reputation is
another ironic touch.] He chose to aid Ulrik out of
obedience to his own inner conviction: " 'I hate
the coward within me,' he said. 'the voice that
whispers counsels of surrender. But if I fled, and
saved this flesh, what spirit would then live on to
light it?' " His humanity and purity of motive as
much as his courage make him a splendid example
of the Northern heroic ideal, which J.R.R. Tolkien
described as "uttermost endurance in the service
of indomitable will."

His destroyer fares otherwise. Condemned to
unrelenting torment by his conscience, Ulrik is
more alone among crowds of pampered pleasure-
seekers than solitary Johnny was on his bleakly
beautiful world. When Johnny asks, " 'Of what
value is a life without truth?' " Ulrik has no answer.
Having learned one too late, he is left forever
dwarfed by a fallen giant.

Thus, worth is a matter of character, not power:
plucky Jimper and steadfast Johnny both walk tall.
Since magnitudes depend on how measurements
are made—and by whom—nothing in a Laumer
story is quite what it seems at first glance. His
universe is continually shifting and eddying around

his unwavering protagonists. Awesome mysteries
may lurk behind commonplace facades. Even the
distinction between illusion and actuality may be a
matter of choice.

For instance, when continents convulse, forgotten chapters in man's preglacial past come to light
in *Catastrophe Planet/The Breaking Earth* [1966].
Geological upheavals are both the source and
symbol of shattering revelations about alien parasites and lost civilizations. Knowledge, as always,
is the margin of survival.

More forgotten prehistory is uncovered in a sex
farce, "The War Against the Yukks" [1965]. But
Laumer recasts history more often than he expands
it. Changing history may be a deliberate effect as
in "Of Death What Dreams" [1970] or a comic
accident as in *The Great Time Machine Hoax*. In
the former story, a powerful mind reaches back
into the past telepathically to right a grievous wrong.
The latter novel, which has been called "a wild
escapade backward, forward, and sideways through
time", deals with inadvertent changes. Careless
use of a sentient super computer sketches and
erases timelines because the images this device
constructs can become real.

The author has lavished particular attention on
parallel world adventures. Here, alternative histo-
ries are coexisting natural phenomena. When communication between them occurs, so does conflict.
Critic Patrick McGuire considers Laumer's "bril-
liantly detailed and remarkably plausible picture of
the 'fabric of simultaneous reality' " to be his most
notable science fictional innovation. Laumer's ver-
sions of crosstime struggle are worthy to stand
beside Jack Williamson's *Legion of Time* [1938],

Poul Anderson's *Guardians of Time* [1960], Fritz Leiber's *Big Time*, as well as efforts by Fred Saberhagen, André Norton, and John Brunner, to cite but a few examples in this genre.

As usual, Laumer presents his subject both seriously and lightly. First came the Imperium trilogy: *Worlds of the Imperium* [1962], *The Other Side of Time* [1965] and *Assignment in Nowhere* [1968]. [The latter two volumes were published by Tor Books under one cover as *Beyond the Imperium*, 1981.] Then these ideas were treated to "gentle parody" in the Lafayette O'Leary series: *The Time Bender* [1966], *The World Shuffler* [1970], and *The Shape-Changer* [1972].

Not only are the Imperium stories the best of this lot, their sheer inventiveness, brisk drama, and sympathetic characters place them among the very best books Laumer has written. The Imperium—or to give its full title, the Anglo-Germanic Imperium—occupies one alternate history line in the total space-time continuum called the Net. Born with the twentieth century, this benevolent, Victorian-flavored empire dominates Earth because it reaps the profits of trade with parallel worlds. It is an urbane, aristocratic society, a place where "the colors were somehow a little brighter, the evening breeze a little softer, the magic of living a little closer." [One may speculate that the author himself would find it an eminently congenial home.]

The Imperium plucks American diplomat Brion Bayard out of our world and, after recruiting him as a Net Surveillance Officer, sends him on missions to other timelines. These feature a wretched, post-holocaust Free French state in North Africa, worlds occupied by loathsome Neanderthals and over-subtle Australopithecines, an enduring Bonapartist French Empire, and a whole tangle of variants determined by the Plantagenet dynasty's actions.

The dynamics of Net travel set forth in *Worlds of the Imperium* are further complicated by time travel in *The Other Side of Time* and quasi-mystical translinear affinities in *Assignment in Nowhere*. The first volume is a gritty straightforward thriller. The second adds sardonic wit and a dazzling display of time paradoxes. The third, with its moral dilemmas and romantic poignancy verges on fantasy. Thus the trilogy is an impressive showcase for Laumer's imagination.

However, the author dramatizes the fluidity of existence even more fantastically in *Night of Delusions* [1972]. Here 1930's hardboiled detective fiction is treated as a body of myth. Down the mean streets of his own mind the hero must go to free himself from a mirror-maze of subjective realities and thereby save his sanity and his world. After solving the mystery and attaining virtual godhood he concludes: " 'Perhaps nothing in life is real. But it doesn't matter. We have to live it as if it were.' "

Pop culture correlatives, metaphysical speculations, a flair for farce, and a pervasive distrust of appearances are some of the traits Laumer shares with Philip K. Dick, the master of mutability. For example, compare *Night of Delusions* with *Ubik* [1969] or *Eye in the Sky* [1956]. All these books depict successive waves of variant realities generated by characters' minds.

The strongest similarity between these two writers is their preoccupation with disguises, illusions, and deceptions of every sort. Both have created delusive—and destructive—alien menaces of unforgettable ghastliness—brain-stealing canines in *A Plague of Demons* [1965] and a half-mechanized messiah in *The Three Stigmata of Palmer Eldritch* [1964]. Significantly, former military officer, Laumer, resolves the issue by force, but pacifist Dick relies on non-violent means.

Laumer's elitism is wholly unlike Dick's preference for "little heroes" as in *The Man in the High Castle* [1962]. While Laumer's protagonists strive to reach beyond themselves, Dick's fear the transcendence that may be thrust upon them: contrast Laumer's *House in November* [1970] with Dick's *Divine Invasion* [1982]. Although working from very different premises, each writer concludes that our universe is simply what our thoughts make it. As Laumer says in *The Great Time Machine Hoax:* " 'The mind is the supreme instrument in nature; it must establish its supremacy.' "

The secret alien invasion [also used by Dick in *Do Androids Dream of Electric Sheep?*, 1968] is a plot at which Laumer excels. [Appropriately, he novelized a television series on that theme called *The Invaders*.] Even in the book at hand, "The Other Sky" is an irony-laden interlace of alien invasions while "Once There Was a Giant" reverses roles with an Earthborn assassin violating another world.

Although Laumer's treatment is usually grim, he gleefully burlesques his own favorite plot in *The Monitors* [1966]. Here, a band of galactic do-gooders tries to force utopia down the human race's throat. [" 'No matter how petty, cruel, blind,

shortsighted, foolish, venal, bloodthirsty, masoch-
istic and obtuse you may be,' '' says the chief
Monitor, " 'it is a matter of principle with us, as
civilized beings, to do our very best to raise you to
our own level of advancement. . . .' ''] Although
their ill-advised charity is angrily refused, they are
later hired to govern Earth on contract.

Whether they arrive openly or secretly, the be-
nevolence alien intruders profess is frequently false,
as in "The Other Sky" and *Night of Delusions*.
Our hidden enemies may be parasites [*Catastrophe
Planet*], manipulators [*The Ultimax Man*, 1978],
exterminators [*The House in November*], or preda-
tors [*A Plague of Demons*].

Whether effete or gross, cunning or dull, extra-
terrestrials who fear humanity's potential make dangerous foes. The dynamism of our species is
universally resented and misunderstood in *Earthblood* [1966]. In *The Ultimax Man*, human progress is routinely thwarted lest it disturb the Galactic Consensus. The hero of *The House in November*
compels a deadly alien hive-mind called the Mone
to repent of its genocide and accept mankind as a
future peer species. In *A Plague of Demons,* Earth
is "an insignificant scintilla" among the stars, its
race "a sinister tribe of barbaric freaks, harvested
like wild honey." Man is a conceptual hybrid
hated as "impure" by both opposing polarities
that eternally war across a dualistic universe.
Nevertheless, being a synthesis of alternative forces
gives Man a potential for ultimate supremacy once
the enslaving spell is broken. The novel's last line
hurls defiance at the ancient foe, "a mighty roar in
many tongues, from many ages—the voice of Man,
that would soon be heard among the stars."

To Laumer, life is a perpetual contest. The conflict may be bloody as battle or genteel as a game. Although physical and mystical clashes are commoner in his work, Laumer's characters also know how to fight with their wits. The sprightly gambling scene in "Of Death What Dreams" reads like futuristic Georgette Heyer. But a worthy foe is needed to give any victory meaning. Man and Mone can come together at the close of *The House in November* precisely because they have first fought. The Mone is forced to acknowledge in conversation what it has already felt in combat. Beyond basic survival, a winner's prize is freedom, freedom to mold the future as in *The Ultimax Man* or to shape the very fabric of existence in *Night of Delusions.*

Since war offers the maximum opportunity for dramatic conflict, it is a frequent setting for Laumer's stories. Whether an old man or a cybernetic juggernaut does the fighting, the scale of the action is always personal, never flattening down to the board-game level.

Personalizing so unlikely an object as a mighty Bolo tank, infusing it with beauty, dignity, virtue— even pathos—is no mean artistic achievement. ["Machinery the Bolos were, but never *mere*."] These colossal, automated, and finally self-aware war machines, Laumer's most popular inventions, are featured in *Bolo* [1976]. This collection, subtitled *The Annals of the Dinochrome Brigade,* traces the development of ever-deadlier models across the centuries. Initially, they were simply formidable weapons. [Compare the supertank in Fred Saberhagen's *Broken Lands,* 1968.] But once they attain sentience, they can die bravely " 'for the

honor of the regiment,' " accept the *coup de grace*
calmly, or reveal aesthetic sensibilities. These sympathetic entities could not be more unlike the life-
hating variety of intelligent war machines typified
by Saberhagen's berserkers. The Bolo who declares:
"I am strong, I am proud, I am capable. I have a
function; I perform it well, and I am at peace with
myself," could be any Laumer hero speaking his
mind. The author's delight in powerful, perfectly
operating mechanisms has never shone clearer.

Because of this enthusiasm, Laumer does not
confine his Bolos to a single universe. One has a
cameo role in *Night of Delusions* and the hero of *A
Plague of Demons* actually *becomes* one. In the
latter novel, loathsome alien invaders create Bolo-
like slave cyborgs operated by living brains stolen
from human warriors over the course of the past
millenium. But once their mental bondage is broken,
the machines turn on their monstrous masters and
destroy them.

This band of chromeplated brothers and the faithful sentry in "Thunderhead" both epitomize mar-
tial valor. Laumer's admiration for the courage
and prowess of fighting men places him in the
company of such sf war chroniclers as Robert A.
Heinlein, Gordon R. Dickson, Jerry Pournelle, and
David Drake. But in Laumer's case, this respect is
coupled with a raging contempt for military chain
of command. [Bungling superiors cause the tragedy in "Thunderhead."] His stories are rife with
tyranny from above and rebellion from below—
each extreme a species of stupidity. This pattern
runs from Laumer's first publication "Greylorn"
[1959] to its recent sequel *Star Colony* [1981].

Nor is it limited to military contexts. Two stints

in the Air Force and three especially bitter years in the Foreign Service have made Laumer an implacable foe of bureaucracy in any form. "It's a concept that has flaws built into it, part of its nature," he says. Since, according to the Peter Principle, bureaucrats are routinely promoted to the level of their incompetence, "you have an incompetent occupying every position." His Hugo Award-nominated story "In the Queue" [1970] is a mordant satire on bureaucratic oppression and the mindset that submits to it.

Such rigid systems allow the inept to shackle the able. Nevertheless, an exceptionally competent man can still manage to prevail against a corrupt and unjust society as in "Of Death What Dreams." Even hydra-headed tyrannies can topple. The heroes of "The Night of the Trolls" [1963], "Worldmaster" [1965], "King of the City" [1961], and *Star Colony* defeat intertwined political, criminal, and military hierarchies. Alien as well as human institutions collect their share of ridicule, notable in *The Ultimax Man* [which also takes a passing jab at Heinlein's *Have Spacesuit—Will Travel,* 1958].

However, diplomatic folly understandably attracts this ex-diplomat's particular ire. Laumer attacks the striped pants set earnestly in his mainstream novel *Embassy,* and comically in his Retief series. The latter, which numbers nearly a dozen volumes published over two decades, includes *Envoy to New Worlds* [1963], *Galactic Diplomat* [1965], and *Retief's War* [1966]. Jame Retief is the one sound man in the bumbling *Corps Diplomatique Terrestrienne,* "a great supra-national organization dedicated to the contravention of war" or, more candidly, "maintenance of a state of tension short of actual conflict." Sean Connery could aptly portray this debonair and omnicompetent hero, but it is said that when the series first appeared, Laumer himself "could make you believe he was Retief."

The favorite character of author and readers alike, Retief is described by his spindle-shanked superior, Magnan, as having an " 'unfortunate tendency to essay japes at the expense of decorum.' " While ever-ready to "vow eternal chum-ship" with reasonable aliens and decent human colonists, Retief tirelessly disarms the snares of slimy or chitinous miscreants before purblind officials with such evocative names as Crodfoller, Hidebinder, and Sternwheeler tumble into the traps. Moreover, he accomplishes his world-saving feats without missing a single pretty girl or good cigar en route. Other professional hazards that Retief surmounts include: idiotic policies, absurd dress codes [puce, maroon, and chartreuse are some of the CDT's favorite colors], obfuscatory jargon, and acronymic organizations [e.g.: MEDDLE, MUDDLE, SCROUNGE, and FLOP]. Real prototypes peep through the comic disguise.

But these delightful stories form an open-ended or "template" series. Retief may change posts but his personality remains constant. Laumer has traced some of his other heroes' growth in wisdom and grace. Maturity may be the natural result of experiencing high adventure as in *Galactic Odyssey, Earthblood* [written with Rosel George Brown], and *Planet Run* [written with Gordon R. Dickson, 1967]. Or superior beings may impose a transformative education against some gawky youth's will as in *The Great Time Machine Hoax* and *The*

Ultimax Man. Improvement may sometimes be consciously sought as in "Of Death What Dreams." However achieved, the self-conquest maturity represents is innately more satisfying than triumph over an external foe.

Thus, whether the hero's superiority is innate or acquired, "the basic Laumer type is the full-formed competent man—sure of himself, resourceful, able to mix easily with all levels of society and to get what he wants out of anyone," observes critic McGuire. The point of many Laumer stories is to place the competent man in exactly the right arena to display his abilities properly.

Himself a thoroughgoing perfectionist, Laumer sees self-perfection as life's highest goal and keenest pleasure. Not even the skies can limit a determined man's reach. *Night of Delusions'* hero soars to giddily godlike heights before deciding to return to the more challenging limitations of the mortal state. In contrast, the heroes of *The Great Time Machine Hoax* and *The Ultimax Man* plan to train others in their amazing skills. This is not altruism— improving the lot of others makes their own lot more comfortable. The petty hoodlum turned "Ultimax Man" discovers the sheer joy of achievement with these conclusions: ". . . Really, it's all so sweet. Simple and sweet. I thought 'work' was a dirty word and spent my life avoiding it, when it's the best there is: to do a job well and know you're doing it. . . ."

Daunting obstacles must be scaled to reach that ultimate serenity. As Laumer himself has stated: "I am more interested in the dramatic suitations in which characters can be put, than in documenting life. . . . The emotion-producing stresses applied to the characters make the story. The rest is, for me, secondary. I am also intrigued by the kinds of stresses men will be put to in situations not of the here and now.''

True to his word, Laumer racks his heroes hard. A typical scenario shows a loner making some alarming discovery which his associates deny. Psychiatric experts dismiss the matter with inane rationalizations. The rightful authorities either cannot or will not act. The hero either gets necessary training from elsewhere or else taps hitherto unsuspected inner resources. After grievous suffering, he prevails. And once having become a superman, he may transcend the entire framework of the original problem.

But Laumer freely admits: ''The plot is nothing—it's what the writer does with the plot and how he does it.'' *The House in November* is a convenient example of how the author dramatizes his basic outline.

The novel opens with successful architectural engineer Jeff Mallory awakening one spring morning to find three months gone from his memory. Waves of wrongness race outward from that initial point of recognition—his appearance, his home, his family, his town have become sorry shadows of their former selves. The scope of the calamity is established through a swarm of details—trivial as spoilt milk, grisly as a shriveled corpse lying on a neighbor's driveway. Mallory verifies that all the other townspeople have been reduced to a zombie-like state by creatures who are ghastly parodies of humankind. [Their preposterous costumes—from cowboy suits to aloha shirts—are part of their tissues, an especially eerie touch.]

Escape brings Mallory no safety because survivors in the surrounding countryside are locked into their own set of delusions and will not heed his testimony. So instead of the expected survival or resistance epic, there is black comedy deploring the blindness of authoritarian minds. [The army commander believes the invaders to be Chinese Communists while a fundamentalist leader holds with equal fervor that they are demons.]

Only after reaching refuge in a derelict mansion out of his own childhood dreams does Mallory get the armament he needs. The Old House—a perpetual November—is a decaying shell that conceals the dazzling hardware of an extraterrestrial observation post. In this place where past and future, ally and betrayer meet, Mallory is infused with sublime powers from beyond the stars. He slashes through a dusty web of lies to uncover the truth about old treacheries that left Earth defenseless against infection by the "living disease" called the Mone.

Returning home, he penetrates the enemy's hive and duels their Queen ere they can multiply. Mallory fortifies himself for the test with the strength of other persons' minds, "spilling out the resident egos as rudely as a starving man shelling oysters." The battlefield report intercuts events and explanations, alternating struggle, victory, tragedy, eucatastrophe, regret, and final, reasoned hope. Green vines hide ruins. Metaphysical grief gives way to clear-skied spring.

Headlong plotting with more turns than a road race make such fantastic adventures believable. Laumer's prose style supports this effect with language that is brisk, direct, and exact. Because he abhors self-indulgent wordplay, he ruthlessly prunes excess verbiage from his text. Images and symbols are held in check although he does permit himself portentious names such as Bravais, Vallant, and Danger. His goal—most perfectly achieved in "Once There Was a Giant"—is to create fiction so hard and tight it brooks no argument.

Judicious set decoration is another means to this end. In close-up, the furnishings of each scene seem properly firm to the touch. Settings are shown in sufficient detail to establish their reality without overwhelming the reader. A Laumer protagonist moves through a world illuminated by a tightbeam spotlight.

The sights thus seen tend to repeat from story to story, whether these take place in the same secondary universe or not. Entirely separate casts of Laumer characters wear polyon clothing, use powerguns, smoke dopesticks, drive Monojag cars, visit Granyauck, or stay in a Railroad Men's YMCA. This complicates the task of sorting out series components. Political and historical references place *Bolo* and *Star Colony* in Retief's universe, despite the wide range of literary forms employed in these works. The term "Ultimax" carries different meanings in *A Plague of Demons* and *The Ultimax Man*; the presence of the vile Niss in both "The Other Sky" and *Earthblood* does not suffice to link these two stories. Nevertheless, the repetition of terminology and names reinforces the common elements in Laumer's plots, thus imposing a tenuous unity on his whole body of fiction. Many of these adventures could be happening in just the sort of parallel worlds network that so often provides their setting. [Similar observations apply to Philip K. Dick's family of subjective universes.]

For immediacy the protagonist through whose eyes these scenes unfold operates in first person or in third person so closely focussed it carries similar force. [*Star Colony* with its multiple viewpoints is an exception.] A consequence of this technique is a lack of self-description. Since the protagonist takes his own appearance for granted, he seldom feels impelled to comment on it. A paucity of detail can stimulate imagination. We are told that Retief—like many another Laumer hero—is six feet, three inches tall. His face is deliberately unpictured yet readers would recognize him on sight.

Actions rather than appearance characterize a Laumer protagonist. Here, deeds do make the man. This is the cornerstone of his approach to fiction. He advises the apprentice writer to "become an actor; act out all your scenes, even to the extent of getting out of your chair and going through the motions, keeping the relationships, both temporal and spatial, of your characters and the objects straight. Speak the dialogue; this alone should be enough to prevent you from having characters deliver four-page lectures to one another, detailing what would be obvious to them if they weren't made of thin cardboard. Live your scenes; BE there, feel, taste, smell, experience."

Laumer rightly emphasizes dialogue because he is uncommonly skilled at writing it. Notice how he recasts his first publication, "Greylorn," a conventional third-person narrative, as an interview in *Star Colony,* with excellent results. Crisp speech, clever slang, and sardonic wit are Laumer trade-

marks. No character wastes time on internal rumi-
nations or mindless chatter. His mastery of dialogue
serves grim or comic purposes equally well. So-
cially nuanced talk in "Of Death What Dreams"
efficently conveys the caste-ridden misery of that
world. A dizzy profusion of native dialects makes
Retief's War a merry romp. In "Once There Was a
Giant," Ulrik's cynicism and Johnny's sincerity
are revealed in the cadence as much as the content
of their spoken words.

Laumer's inborn gift for dialogue was further
trained by meticulous study of his literary idol,
Raymond Chandler, the master of hardboiled detective fiction. The influence extends beyond dialog
technique. His fondness for Chandleresque figures
of speech yields colorful sentences such as: "Her
bosom swung over him like a pair of impending
dooms." Although *Night of Delusions* is his spe-
cific homage to the great mystery writer, Laumer
emulates his model's terseness and concreteness in
every story.

Veneration of Chandler is but one private preference evident in Laumer's writing. "Everything I
ever read, everything that ever happened to me,
influenced me," he says. Moreover, he admits
that "unless the writer is a cold-blooded hack,
churning out stuff between yawns, he reveals himself fully in his work—with the exception of those
personal faults of which he is conscious and suc-
ceeds in concealing."

His perfectionism has already been noted.
" 'Everything properly made and perfectly maintained,' seems to be his motto" according to inter-
viewer Charles Platt who describes Laumer as a
man of "formidable intellect and not a shred of

false modesty. . . . He had taught himself something about almost everything, from history to language to gourmet cooking to engineering to art. . . . He showed a small amount of pity and a fair amount of scorn for anyone who was less demanding than he was—as though he believed excellence was the only value that truly mattered.''

By all accounts, the multi-talented and acutely class-conscious Laumer is devoted to high standards and rigorous discipline. These traits were honed by military service and education as an architectural engineer. [He received his bachelor's degree from the University of Illinois in 1952.] Like his heroes, he is a man who likes ''solid and familiar luxury''—in both his dinner and his dinner table. He designed a beautiful home for himself in the Florida woods and filled it with furniture of his own making. Surely the reverie about an ideal house in *The Ultimax Man* expresses the author's own aspirations: '' 'I have labored to create here the optimum blending of beauty with utility. . . . Here nothing was left to chance, every atom was planned; there has been no compromise with ease or cheapness; all is of the finest and is maintained flawlessly.' ''

Laumer also admires elegance in dress. His hero's delight at the gold-braided splendor of an officer's uniform in *Worlds of the Imperium* might be his own: ''This outfit made a man look like a man. How the devil had we gotten into the habit of draping ourselves in shapeless double-breasted suits in mousy colors, of identical cut?'' This craving for color can also yield humor, as in CDT diplomats' silly garb. [Note Retief's dazzling disguise as an organo-metallic arthropod in *Retief's War*.]

Vehicles are another Laumer enthusiasm. He restores old automobiles as a pastime, and once considered turning a classic Lincoln he owned into a sort of time machine by filling it with period artifacts. [Were it but practical, one might imagine him trying to build a Bolo tank.] The knowledge of aircraft that went into his hobby book, *How to Design and Build Flying Models* was thriftily recycled in the glider episode of *The Great Time Machine Hoax*.

The unusual attention Laumer lavishes on training sequences in his fiction, for example in *The Ultimax Man* and "Of Death What Dreams", expresses his pride in past learning accomplishments and his confidence in possibilities yet unrealized. " 'Each entity, living or inert, has its own potential; to fulfill that potential is to perfect the entity.' " A man makes himself what he is and creates the world he chooses to live in. " 'You can't find your dreamworld by packing up and moving on; you've got to build it where you are.' "

In the endless quest for fulfillment, striving is its own reward. As Laumer concludes in *Night of Delusions:*

"Success is the challenge nobody's ever met. Because no matter how many you win, there's always a bigger and harder and more complicated problem ahead, and there always will be, and the secret isn't Victory Forever but to keep on doing the best you can one day at a time and remember you're a Man, not just god, and for you there aren't and never will be any easy answers, only questions, and no reasons, only causes, and no meaning, only intelligence, and no destination and no kindly magic smiling down from above, and no fires to goad you from below, only Yourself and the Universe and what You make out of the interface between the two equals.''